The War Rages On

CECELIA SCHMIDT

Author's Note

Although *The War Rages On* is set against the backdrop of the
War Between the States (Civil War), it was not written with any
intent to represent either of the two sides involved in the war.
All characters and events are fictitious and any resemblance to
real persons or events, living or dead, is purely coincidental.

Dedication

Dedicated to my beloved family and dearest friends, who have
continually helped and encouraged me during the writing of this
book. But above all others, I dedicate this to my
Lord and Savior Jesus Christ.

A special thanks to Pamela White and Julia LoVullo.

Praise for
The War Rages On

"A wonderful, wholesome book. Just what I would want my daughter to read."

–Dionne W, homeschool mom of four

"It was such a great book! I was sad every time I had to put it down and go back to real life!"

–Sarah, age 16

"*The War Rages On* clearly portrays God's blessings, some in the past to be cherished, some in the future to wait for, but most of all, some right now to enjoy. This book has encouraged me to treasure and love my sister more."

–Kay, age 14

CONTENTS

CHAPTER ONE

THE PREACHER'S SON

"Grace, where are you going?" Mrs. Johnson questioned her daughter.

"Mrs. Carver asked if I could join them for supper tonight," Grace answered with a smile on her beautiful face.

"But you were just over there last week."

"Mrs. Carver says they all enjoy having me. May I please go?"

Mrs. Johnson stared at her excited daughter. Looking into those sparkling eyes, she remembered that Grace was not a little girl anymore. She was sixteen years old and less than a year away from the time her father said she may get married.

"Oh, alright. But don't be home late. I'll have your father take you over in the wagon."

"There's really no need, Ma. I can ride over there myself."

Just then, Grace's father came in from the barn. His clothes were a mess and his hair all disheveled.

"That stubborn cow won't give any milk again! The only thing she's good for is a side of beef!" Mr. Johnson stopped talking when he spotted Grace adding the final touch to her hair.

"Where are you going, young lady?" he asked gruffly.

"Over to the Carvers' place. Mrs. Carver asked me over for supper," Grace replied. She knew how her father felt about her visiting "that blasted preacher's son" as he called the Carvers' son, David.

"Really, Grace! Why do you have to go visiting that

blasted preacher's son? He's going to grow up to be just like his father! All preachin' and prayin' like," Mr. Johnson snarled.

Then, turning to his wife, he questioned, "Clara, what are we going to do with this girl?"

However, one look at Grace, and he relented.

"Oh, fine. Just go, but don't be home late!"

"Thank you, Father. I won't be home late. I promise."

Grace quickly left the house before her father changed his mind. She saddled her horse, Violet, and rode off toward David's house.

"She's not your little girl anymore, Tom. You said yourself that she could marry when she was seventeen years old," Mrs. Johnson reminded her husband.

"I know, but out of all the boys around, why does she have to be sweet on David Carver?"

"He's a nice boy," Grace's sister, Rebekah, added as she came out of her parents' room. Rebekah was ten years old and very frail. Sickness regularly overcame her. When Rebekah was younger, Mr. and Mrs. Johnson had decided that it would be a good idea if they moved her out of the room that she and Grace had shared and into their room. Since she was sick so often, Mrs. Johnson wanted to be near her in case she needed help during the night.

"Rebekah, what are you doing out of bed?" her mother questioned.

"I heard you talking about David."

"Sweetie, you know you have to stay in bed. Doctor Hays said that if you want to get better you need to rest," her mother gently replied.

"It gets lonesome in that bed all day."

"I know, Rebekah, but you *need* to rest."

"Your mother's right, Rebekah. Now go back to bed, and from now on, don't interrupt adult conversations," Mr. Johnson spoke up.

"Yes, sir," Rebekah sighed as she reluctantly obeyed.

* * *

At the Carvers' cabin, Grace ate heartily and talked merrily. When their conversation had come to a close, Grace stood up and thanked Mrs. Carver for the meal.

"I'm glad you enjoyed it, Grace. You're always welcome here," Mrs. Carver kindly responded.

"I'd like to ride over to your place with you, Grace. I need to talk with your folks," David suddenly remarked.

"Alright," Grace replied. She couldn't help but wonder if this would be the night that David would ask her father for permission to marry her.

As they rode over the hill, Grace, convinced of what David's intentions were, playfully asked, "So what do you want to talk to my folks about?"

He tauntingly responded back, "Well, that's between me and them."

They laughed and talked, and it seemed like only a moment before they arrived at Grace's cabin.

Mrs. Johnson met them at the door while Mr. Johnson pretended not to notice the unwanted visitor.

"Good evening, ma'am," David said politely with a warm smile.

"Hello, David. May I get you something to drink?" Mrs. Johnson tried to make him feel welcome.

"No, thank you, ma'am. I came here on some important

business." He signaled with his eyes that he would like to speak about whatever it was alone without Grace present.

Mrs. Johnson took the hint. "Oh, well, Grace how about you go into your room and get ready for bed."

"Yes, Ma. Goodnight David," Grace complied.

"Goodnight, Grace," he tenderly responded.

Once she had left, David turned his attention to the solemn man, who sat rocking in his chair by the fire, smoking his pipe. Without hesitation, he announced, "Mr. Johnson, I came here to ask for permission to marry your daughter."

Mr. Johnson finally looked up at David and rather kindly responded, "Why don't we go outside."

David nodded in agreement.

Outside, David and Mr. Johnson walked over near the barn and leaned up against the wooden fence. The stars shone brightly as the two of them stood in silence for a few moments. Then, Mr. Johnson spoke.

"She's rather young, David."

"I know, sir. I'm willing to wait until she comes of age to take her as my wife."

"I told her she could marry when she turns seventeen." Mr. Johnson scanned the figure of the young man. "How old are you?"

"Seventeen, sir."

Mr. Johnson turned his head away from David and thought for a few moments. The thought of David's being a preacher's son troubled him.

"I don't know, David. I'd like to discuss this with my wife before I make my decision."

Disappointed yet retaining his dignity, David quietly

consented, "Yes, sir. Good night." David tipped his hat to Mr. Johnson and started to get on his horse.

"Your daughter's a wonderful young lady, and I'd sure be proud to have her as my wife," David added.

"Thank you." Mr. Johnson watched as David rode away. His mind swirled with a million different thoughts about both Grace and David. He stood there for a while, just thinking. Finally, the chilly wind nipped at his cheeks, interrupting his thoughts, and he went back into the cabin to join his wife.

*   *   *

"He's a kind and thoughtful boy, Tom. He'd be a great husband for Grace," Clara appealed to her anxious husband.

"But he's a preacher's son! I don't want Grace being tied up in all that church and God stuff."

"And why not?"

"What?"

"What's so bad about all that 'church and God stuff?' You knew when you married me that I was a Christian and had been brought up in the same kind of home as David. You told me that I was allowed to believe what I wanted as long as I left you alone about it, and haven't I? Haven't I left you alone about it up until now?"

"Yes."

"Grace thinks quite differently about Christianity than you do. If she found it all to be nonsense, she wouldn't have become a Christian. A preacher's son would be the best thing for her."

"I don't want my daughter—"

"If you want your daughter to have a blessed and joyful marriage, you should allow her to marry that boy."

Mr. Johnson paused for a moment and stared out the window into the starry sky.

"I love my little girl. I just—"

He turned to his wife, looked into her bright blue eyes, and chose not to finish what he was going to say.

"Good night," he said calmly. He walked into their bedroom and shut the door behind him.

A minute later, Grace came out of her room.

"Ma, why doesn't father like David? He's the kindest young man I've ever known."

"You know your father is against Christianity, Grace. He doesn't mind my following after God, but he hates the idea of you marrying a man so devoted to the Lord as David."

"But isn't being devoted to God a good thing?"

"Of course it is. Your father just doesn't see it that way, although I pray that one day he will."

"But Ma, if you knew that Father was against Christianity from the start, why did you marry him?"

A look of regret came into Mrs. Johnson's eyes.

"I was no older than you when your father came into my life. I was so smitten with him. When he asked me to marry him, I said 'yes' right away without any hesitation. I was too overwhelmed and excited to think about what I had been taught my whole life."

"But if your parents knew that Father proposed, why didn't they stop him?"

Mrs. Johnson turned her head away as the painful memories rushed back to her.

"They didn't know. We just ran off and got married."

Grace let out a gasp. She was shocked. She never knew.

How could her mother do something like that? How could she go against everything she had ever been taught?

"Why?"

"I was afraid that if I told my parents, they wouldn't let me see your father anymore. I regret that now. I wish I had made things right."

"Well, you still could. Why don't you go to them? Go and—"

"They're both dead."

Grace backed away from her mother. She felt faint. All of this was coming on her at once. It was just too much.

"But all this time I just thought they lived too far away for us to visit them. How did they die?"

"Not long after I left, my mother came down with malaria. She died a few days later."

"And what about grandfather?"

"After my mother died, he was so brokenhearted. His only child had run away and never come back. Now his wife was dead, and he was all alone. He had a heart attack as he was farming one day, and a neighbor found him out in the field."

The memories were just too much for Mrs. Johnson, and she burst into tears.

"Oh, Ma, please don't cry. We all make mistakes. Their deaths weren't your fault."

"But if I had only listened. If only I had gone back! Then, I would have gotten to say I was sorry. I could have made things right. That is why, Grace—" Mrs. Johnson paused for a moment and stroked Grace's long hair. "That is why I want you to marry David. He's a good, Christian man, and I see in him all the qualities that my parents wanted me to look for in a husband. He's kind, gentle, hard-working, thoughtful, and devoted to Christ. If anyone is to marry you, I want it to be him."

The tears started streaming down Grace's cheeks. She was so filled with joy that her mother wanted her to marry David.

"But what about Father? You know he doesn't want me to marry him. But I can't stand the thought of marrying anyone else."

"Don't worry, dear. I had a good talk with your father earlier tonight. I think he may be willing if we just give him a chance. Don't push him. In the meantime, don't make any foolish choices. Be patient and listen to the advice that you are given. Don't be like me, Grace. Please don't be like me!" Mrs. Johnson pulled Grace close to her, and they stood for a long time, hugging one another.

CHAPTER 2

THE MILLERS

The following morning, Mr. Johnson came to the breakfast table. His countenance revealed he had something weighing on his mind. Grace and Mrs. Johnson looked at each other and exchanged similar glances. They both knew what was troubling him. Rebekah, unaware of the situation, sat quietly, keeping any comments that she might have had to herself.

"Did you sleep well, Father?" Grace asked.

"Well enough."

"Eggs, dear?" Mrs. Johnson added.

"Thank you," Mr. Johnson replied, his mood having not changed a bit.

The family ate their breakfast in almost complete silence except for a few comments from Mrs. Johnson here and there about the harvest dance that was coming soon. Folks in the area would get together and celebrate the harvest.

"I hear that the new family, the Millers, will be there. I had a chance to meet Mrs. Miller in the mercantile a few days ago. She's a very nice woman," Mrs. Johnson relayed.

Mr. Johnson, his mind having been a little relieved of the stress from the night before, finally spoke.

"I had a chance to meet Mr. Miller at the blacksmith's shop a little while ago. Seems like a good a man." Turning towards Grace, he added, "He has a boy about your age, Grace. Thomas, I think his name is."

"That's nice," Grace gently responded.

"Good boy, I hear. Hard worker like his father. You'd like

him, Grace." Mr. Johnson paused for a moment. An idea struck him.

"Clara, I think we should invite them over for supper."

Mrs. Johnson looked at Grace, who in turn looked at her father with surprise. Rebekah looked up from her plate, also wondering what her father was up to.

"But we hardly know them," Grace nervously responded. She didn't want a boy her age being pushed into her life by her father.

"Nonsense! What better way to get to know a family than by inviting them over to eat and talk? Clara, when you go into town tomorrow morning, invite them over to supper this week."

"I'll try to, dear. I don't know if I'll see Mrs. Miller or not, but if I do, I'll be sure to ask," Mrs. Johnson apprehensively answered.

"Good."

With that, everyone continued eating their breakfast. Grace felt sick to her stomach. She knew what her father was doing. He wanted her and Thomas to get to know one another so that she could forget about David. She never could. What could she say? How could she tell her father how she felt? She decided that to say nothing would be the best option for now.

The next day, Mrs. Johnson, Grace, and Rebekah rode into town, talking the whole ride there. Grace enjoyed every moment of it. She loved being with her sister, but she especially enjoyed the quality time she spent with her mother. They were both women and understood each other's feelings like no one else could. Grace cherished her mother more than anyone else. There was a bond between them that could not be broken. So it should be with all mothers and daughters.

As Grace rode in the wagon beside her mother, her mind swirled with thoughts about the past few months, troubling thoughts. July was coming to a close. Sadly, a war had been taking place for almost four months now, a war between the states. The country was divided over the issue of slavery. Grace did not fully understand all the details, but she knew that she did not approve of the idea of one person owning another. She hoped that the war would be over soon and that nothing would ever cause division like this again.

When the town finally came into view, Grace quietly asked her mother, "What if Mrs. Miller is in town and accepts the invitation. What do I do? You know Father is just trying to get the Millers over because of me. He wants me to focus my attention on some other boy, but I just can't!"

"Grace, if the Millers do end up coming, just be yourself. Don't let the Millers know you're unhappy. Tell your father in private how you feel."

"Alright, I'll just be myself, and when they leave, I *will* tell Father how I feel. I don't want to be pushed into a marriage with someone I don't love."

"I agree, Grace, and I promise that you won't be. I don't think your father would go as far as forcing you to marry Thomas. He may be stubborn at times, but he's not cruel. Besides, as a non-Christian he looks at things differently than we do."

The wagon pulled up in front of the mercantile, and they all got out.

"Alright, Grace, would you see if there's any mail for us?" Mrs. Johnson asked. "I just have a few things to grab, and then we'll head back home."

"Yes, Ma." Grace obeyed.

Mrs. Johnson took Rebekah's hand, and together they walked up the steps into the mercantile. Grace took care of the horses and situated her bonnet on her head. She walked through town and looked all around her. It was a quiet town for the most part. There was a small white post office and a school house nearby. The mercantile was small as well, but it provided everything that someone in the country would need. Not far away stood the doctor's office. Grace loved Doctor Hays because he gave Rebekah and her candy every time they went to see him. Across the street there was a lumber mill and next to that, a blacksmith's shop. And last, but certainly not least, was the church. Up until a few years ago, the school building had also served as the church. But with the growing congregation, it had gotten too crowded. It was Grace's favorite building in town. Situated away from all the noise and bustle, it stood gracefully and had a look about it that made Grace feel at peace. Beside the church stood a large oak tree that Grace adored. Every time she saw it, a flood of wonderful memories rushed through her mind: picnics with friends and family after services and the time when Ethan Jones had gotten stuck in its branches while she and Ethan's older sister, Anna, sat beneath him, laughing at his helplessness. Grace stood, gazing at the beautiful tree as the seconds rolled by. But suddenly, her mind switched from daydreaming to the task before her.

At the post office Grace met the postwoman with a smile.

"Hello, Mrs. Davis," she joyfully greeted.

"Why, hello, Grace. How have you been?"

"Very well, thank you, Mrs. Davis. Is there any mail for us?"

"I don't think so, but I'll check for you."

Mrs. Davis looked behind the counter for any mail that she might have missed.

"Well, dear, nothing today. I'm not surprised, though. Mail's been pretty slow these days. You know, with the war and all."

"Really?"

"Yes, and I'm telling you, we Virginians know where we stand on the issue of slavery, and no amount of fighting is going to change our minds! Those Negros should stay in their place. In the fields are where they belong. We whites shouldn't have to share our rights with those Negros! Can you image all the problems that would arise if they were set free? If you ask me, slaves are what they're good for and nothing else!"

Grace was startled at Mrs. Davis's harsh language and felt uncomfortable.

"Well, thank you, Mrs. Davis. Have a nice day."

With that, Grace quickly left the post office. She was shocked. How could people be so heartless? Why were whites any better than blacks?

"Grace," Mrs. Johnson called out, "I'm done now. Ready the horses and get in the wagon, please."

Grace obediently followed her mother's instructions.

"Did you see Mrs. Miller?" Grace nervously asked.

"Yes, I did. She said that they would be happy to join us. They're coming Friday night at six o'clock."

"Do they have any other children besides Thomas?"

"Yes, a little girl about Rebekah's age. I saw her today. She came right up to me and introduced herself with a big smile on her face. They seem like a nice family, Grace. I think you'll like them."

"Did she say the *whole* family would be coming?"

"Yes, of course. What a silly question, Grace."

"Well, I was just kind of hoping that—"

Mrs. Johnson looked into her daughter's eyes.

"That Thomas wouldn't be able to come?" she finished Grace's statement.

"Yes."

"Grace, it will be alright. Remember, be yourself. Make it a good time, not a bad one," Mrs. Johnson replied gently.

"I'll do my best."

Well, Friday night came soon enough. Everyone was all dressed up. Company was rare, and since only Mrs. Johnson and the girls went to church, Mr. Johnson didn't have any nice clothes until his wife had bought some for him the day before.

"How can men stand to wear these?" Mr. Johnson grumbled. "This tie is choking me to death! And this dumb shirt! Why do I have to wear these, Clara?"

"I've told you a thousand times, Tom! We're having company over, and it was your idea to have company over, and, therefore, my good man, you are going to look your best!"

Mr. Johnson let out a sigh and rolled his eyes.

"Besides, you ought to have some nice clothes on hand in case we start having company over more often," Mrs. Johnson stated matter-of-factly.

"Well, if I have to get this dressed up every time we have company over, I'm not sure I wanna make this a normal occurrence!"

"Oh, Tom, it's not that bad," Mrs. Johnson gently corrected

her husband.

Mr. Johnson moaned and tugged at his tie.

A minute later, Rebekah came out of her room, wearing her Sunday best. With her long, dirty-blond hair and brown eyes, she was a sight to behold.

"You look beautiful, Rebekah," Mrs. Johnson told her adorable daughter.

"Thank you, Mama," she humbly replied. She went over to Mr. Johnson, who was smoking his pipe, and sat down on his lap. Hannah, her straw doll, sat with them, too, for Rebekah didn't like for her to be left out of anything.

Grace shortly followed.

"My goodness, Grace, you look ravishing!" Mrs. Johnson exclaimed.

Mrs. Johnson had just finished making the dress Grace was wearing. Grace had outgrown her other two Sunday dresses, so they had been given to Rebekah. This dress in particular was stunning. It was lavender and came just a little above Grace's ankles. The sleeves were elbow length, and ruffles of white lace adorned the cuffs. It was a simple yet elegant dress. Grace's long brunette hair was pulled back in a low bun, making her look much older than when she wore her hair down or in braids. Besides all these things, her hazel eyes were sparkling, completing her striking complexion.

"Thank you, Ma. I love the dress. It's beautiful!" Grace exuberantly thanked her mother.

"You're more than welcome, dear. Do you like the sleeves? I didn't know if you would since all your other dresses had longer ones."

"Oh, no, I love them! They're something different."

"That's what I thought. And I'm glad you've started to pull your hair back. You're past the age of braids now."

"I know. It's not as comfortable, but I'm starting to get used to it."

"Well, it looks lovely," Mrs. Johnson complimented.

"Thank you."

"Your mother's right, Grace," Mr. Johnson commented. "You're a sight to see. Thomas—I mean the Millers—will be very pleased."

Grace looked at her mother, who in turn gave her one of those looks that said, "Don't say anything!"

Grace simply responded, "Thank you, Father."

"I wish I had a dress like Grace's," Rebekah muttered, frowning.

"You will, Rebekah. When you're sixteen, I'll make you a dress just like that in any color you want," Mrs. Johnson told her.

"Sixteen? That's too far away," Rebekah groaned, gazing wishfully at Grace's dress. "I wish I was older like Grace."

"Don't rush it, Rebekah," Mr. Johnson butted in. "You never get these years back."

Rebekah sighed as she moved Hannah meaninglessly here and there. As Mrs. Johnson and Grace went over to the stove to keep preparing dinner, Mr. Johnson leaned his head down next to Rebekah.

"At least you don't have to wear a blasted tie that chokes you to death," he whispered.

Rebekah giggled, and Mrs. Johnson looked up from the stove of goodies.

"What are you two up to?" she asked, curious.

"Nothing. Just talking," Mr. Johnson casually responded. He quickly got up and trying to change the subject, asked, "Do you need any help?"

"No, I think I'm fine. But if you'd like, I can loosen your tie a little bit for you." Adjusting Mr. Johnson's tie, she mocked, "Just so it doesn't choke you to death."

Mr. Johnson gave Rebekah an "oops!" look, and she giggled again.

Soon enough, the Millers arrived. Mr. Johnson helped Mr. Miller and Thomas take care of the horses while the women all went inside.

"It's so nice to finally have you over," Mrs. Johnson told Mrs. Miller.

"Yes, thank you for inviting us. You have a lovely family. Lillian, why don't you help Mrs. Johnson with the table?"

"Ok, Mama," Lillian said. She was a bright and charming eleven-year-old.

When the men came in from the barn, everyone sat down at the dinner table. Once the food was served, there was much eating and talking. Everyone was having a jolly time until Mr. Miller brought up the war.

"How do you feel about slavery, Tom?" Mr. Miller asked.

Mr. Johnson, not wanting to offend his wife, who was against the injustice of slavery, responded, "I'm not quite sure. What about you?"

"I'm all for slavery. After all, if the Negros are set free, can you imagine all the trouble they'd cause us whites? All those illiterate Negros being able to have the same kind of jobs as we whites have. And the more jobs they get, the fewer jobs for us. Then, who would look after all those plantations? I mean, someone's gotta do all the planting and harvesting, and it can't be us. I'm telling you, the only thing those slaves are good for is work and lots of it! Best they just mind themselves and not go messing with us!"

"Well, now that you put it that way—"

"And what do you think about those Virginians who actually support the Negros' cause?" Mr. Miller interrupted.

"Like who?"

"That Carver family, for instance. I'll tell you! That man doesn't have any common sense! All preachin' and prayin'. I ran into him in town yesterday. Most stubborn man I ever met! Won't even think about the issue. He just says, 'Slavery is wrong because all human beings were created equal in God's sight.' Hah! How much more insane can you get? That man's going to get himself into a lot of trouble soon if he doesn't keep his mouth shut! I don't know about you, but I don't like when preachers go around spewing their dangerous ideas on other people. He's gonna pay for it if he doesn't stop!" Mr. Miller exclaimed.

"More coffee, Mr. Miller?" Mrs. Johnson asked, trying to change the subject.

"No, thank you, ma'am. I'm telling you, Tom. Our country won't be safe until we've rid ourselves of every one of his kind!"

Mr. Johnson nodded his head. He looked at Grace, who had been watching him from the stove the entire time. He gave her a look that told her, "I told you that you shouldn't be hanging around the likes of David Carver!"

After dinner, Mrs. Miller and Mrs. Johnson took care of the dishes while Lillian and Rebekah played with their dolls. The men sat talking, sipping their coffee all the while.

Grace, feeling rather restless, wrapped her shawl around her and headed outside to get some fresh air. When he saw Grace leaving, Thomas followed her.

Grace leaned up against the wooden fence besides the barn. She looked out into the sunset and let the beauty of the night sink in.

"What are you doing?" Thomas asked abruptly.

Grace turned sharply around, surprised to find that someone had followed her out.

"I'm sorry. I didn't mean to frighten you," he apologized.

"That's alright," she responded.

Thomas walked over next to Grace and placed his arms on the fence beside her.

"You have a nice family," Thomas told Grace.

"Thank you. So do you," Grace replied.

Their eyes met, and Grace quickly turned away. What would David say if he saw them together?

*   *   *

Over at the Carvers' house, Mrs. Carver instructed David, "Now, I want you to take this jam over to Grace. I know how much she likes it, so I made some extra this time. Be sure to hurry back. Don't stay unless you're asked."

"Yes, ma'am," David respectfully responded. He put the jar into his pack, strapped it onto his horse, and rode off.

*   *   *

"So how old are you?" Thomas asked Grace, who was feeling uneasy at this point.

"Sixteen," Grace replied.

"I'm seventeen." There was a slight pause, and then Thomas asked, "Are you going to the harvest dance?"

Grace's face turned red. She wanted so badly to tell Thomas that someone else had already asked to marry her. She knew it would be rude not to respond, so she quickly replied, "I'm not sure."

"Well, I'd be more than happy to take you as my partner."

"I don't know...." Grace stopped short in the middle of her sentence. This couldn't be happening! Riding over the hill was David.

CHAPTER 3

SPOKEN FOR

David saw them together. He looked at Grace and then quickly rode away. He was over the hill in a second.

"Will you please excuse me?" Grace asked worriedly.

She dashed into the house, leaving Thomas perplexed at what had just happened. She ran straight to her room and shut the door behind her. Leaning up against the wall to stabilize herself, she shook all over with apprehension.

"Oh! What must he think?" Grace rebuked herself over and over again. Mrs. Johnson soon entered the room and sat down on the bed besides Grace.

"What happened, dear?"

"Oh, Ma! I went outside to get a breath of fresh air, and then Thomas came out and he started talking to me, and he invited me to go as his partner to the harvest dance and—"

"Grace, slow down."

"Oh, it's just terrible! David saw us talking together, and Thomas *was* standing awfully close to me."

"It's alright, dear. David is sure to understand once you tell him."

"I know. It's just, I'm sure David was going to ask me to go to the harvest dance with him. That's probably why he was riding over here."

"You might be right, Grace. Although, David shouldn't jump to conclusions as he did."

Grace laid her head against her pillow as the tears rolled down her cheeks.

"This is exactly what Father wanted to happen. Now David's upset!" cried Grace.

"Shhh. Don't cry. It'll be alright, Grace. Listen, it's too dark to ride over there tonight, and it would be impolite to leave with the Millers here. Tomorrow, you can ride over and talk to David. For now, though, I think it would be best to decline Thomas's invitation."

Mrs. Johnson smoothed Grace's long hair and smiled at her.

"I thought love was supposed to be wonderful, Ma, not full of worries and trouble."

"Love is wonderful, Grace, when it's done in the right way. That's why it's so important to not make any foolish choices that you'll regret later on."

Mrs. Johnson gave her daughter a kiss, and they both walked back into the kitchen. Thomas, who was quite puzzled at Grace's flight, was standing against the wall, listening to the fathers talk.

"Thomas, I'm sorry for running off like that," Grace confessed.

"It's alright." There was a slight pause, and then Thomas continued. "I meant what I said about the dance and all. I would be delighted to take you as my partner."

Grace, her heart pounding, answered, "Thomas, I'm spoken for, actually. I appreciate your invitation, but I'm afraid I'll have to decline."

Thomas looked at her, disappointed, and quietly murmured, "I understand."

* * *

The next day, Grace awoke refreshed from the strain of

the night before. She quickly got dressed, grabbed her bonnet, and hurried into the kitchen.

"My, someone's up early!" exclaimed Mrs. Johnson as Grace rushed over to give her a good morning hug and kiss.

"I'm anxious to get over and talk to David."

"I bet you are. But first, eat your breakfast."

With that, Mrs. Johnson set a plate of bacon, eggs, and a biscuit in front of Grace.

What if David doesn't even want to see me? What if he doesn't invite me to the dance, and then I have no partner after all? Grace thought. She pondered on what she would say to David and how she would explain everything.

After she had finished, Grace got up from her seat, thanked her mother for breakfast, and rushed out the door. She saddled up Violet and rode away over the hill.

Upon arriving at David's house, she dismounted and tied Violet to the fence post. As soon as she turned around, there was David, walking out of the barn. Their eyes met, and Grace hurried over to him.

"David, I'm here to talk about last night. Nothing you saw is what you think. The Millers are a new family, and they came over to dinner. They have a son who is your age, and I felt uncomfortable with the situation. So after dinner I walked outside to get some fresh air, and Thomas, the boy I told you about, followed me out, and he got to asking me all these questions like how old I was and if I was going to the dance. He had just invited me to be his partner when you rode over the hill and saw us together. I knew you would take it the wrong way."

David was leaning up against the barn wall and had been

carefully listening to Grace's story.

"I'm telling the truth, David. Honest I am! I don't care for Thomas in the least bit."

David looked at her with eyes full of regret, and then slowly walked over to her. He set his hands on her shoulders and replied, "I believe you, Grace."

"You do?"

"Yes. I got to thinking last night. You've always been loyal to me, and I shouldn't have thought that you would have done something like that. I know it was wrong for me to ride off. I was going to come see you this morning and talk it over just as you arrived. Will you forgive me for leaving like I did?"

"Of course."

David smiled as he looked into her eyes full of compassion. He got down onto his knees, took Grace's hands in his and asked, "Grace Johnson, will you do me the honor of allowing me to escort you to the harvest dance?"

A smile shone on Grace's face as she joyfully responded, "Yes, I will."

David arose. He offered his arm, and Grace took it. They strode for a while, talking about their hopes for the future.

As they got farther away from the house, their conversation shifted to more sorrowful matters. The division of the nation lay heavily on both of their consciences.

"David, your father is making people angry with his preaching about the equality of slaves. Could you please talk to him and ask him to stop? I don't want your family getting hurt." Grace worriedly asked.

"He won't stop no matter what the dangers are. He believes it's his duty as God's ambassador to defend those who cannot defend themselves, just as Christ did."

"But he's causing more trouble. This is Virginia! There are few others who think the way we do. I'm afraid something awful is going to happen. Mr. Miller was talking about your father last night, and he didn't sound pleased. I think he's going to take matters into his own hands soon."

"I hope it never comes to that. After all, Father's just doing what he believes is right."

"Well, not all people see him that way. He needs to be careful."

CHAPTER 4

A FIERY BLAZE

Three weeks slowly rolled by. David warned his father about what Grace had said, but Mr. Carver would not heed David's advice. Each week, he took his place at the pulpit and strongly spoke out against the injustice that was being done to the Negros.

"We may suffer for doing what's right, David. Preaching the truth and standing up for the oppressed is exactly what Jesus did, and I will continue to do the same," Mr. Carver told his son one evening. Sadly, this was an unpopular opinion in Virginia, but the Carvers held to their beliefs, making enemies along the way.

*   *   *

The harvest dance finally arrived. Everyone was bustling about, trying to get everything done. Mrs. Johnson made several pies like she did every year, including her blue-ribbon rhubarb pie, which she was well known for throughout the countryside. Grace was so excited! Every year she waited eagerly for the dance to come.

It was around four o'clock when a knock was heard at the Johnson's door. It was David. He was dressed in his Sunday best, and a handsome smile adorned his face. His dark hair was nicely combed, and his blue eyes were shining.

"Come in, David. How are you?" Mrs. Johnson greeted her favorite guest.

"Very fine, thank you, ma'am. How about yourself?"

"I couldn't be better. I'll go tell Grace you're here."

"Thank you."

Mr. Johnson was in the bedroom getting ready while all of this was taking place. In spite of his negative feelings towards David, he had reluctantly agreed to allow Grace to attend the dance with him.

"Grace." Mrs. Johnson entered Grace's room where she was just adding one final touch to her hair. "David is here."

"I'll be right out. Just let me grab my bag."

Mother and daughter walked out of the room together, and when David laid eyes on Grace, a sense of pride came over him, not a selfish pride but one of esteem. Grace was as beautiful on the inside as she was on the outside.

"Are you ready to go, Grace?" David gently asked her.

"Yes." Hesitantly, she continued. "Just let me say goodbye to my father."

David nodded. Grace gently knocked on the bedroom door, and a gruff voice from inside responded, "Come in."

Grace quietly walked in as Mr. Johnson finished buttoning his shirt.

"Father, David is here. I just wanted to say goodbye."

Mr. Johnson slowly turned and looked at his daughter. Doing his best to be pleasant towards Grace, he softly said to her, "We'll see you at the dance, then."

Grace gave him a hug and left the bedroom. She and David quickly left.

"I hope Grace and David get married soon," Rebekah told her mother.

"Me too, sweetheart, but the war has added strife between your father and the Carvers. If anything like that is going to happen, it probably won't occur for a while."

*   *   *

Once they arrived at the dance, David helped Grace down from the wagon. Many families were there. Grace was secretly hoping that the Millers wouldn't show up and was disappointed when she spotted their wagon.

Everyone was bringing all kinds of wonderful food and desserts. However, none of the pies could compare to Mrs. Johnson's. They were unmatched both in looks and in taste, and everyone knew it.

Standing by the dessert table, the youngest of the Jones boys, Grant, was stuffing numerous cookies into his pockets, hoping that his mother wouldn't notice. The other three, Ethan, Luke, and Matthew, were running about playing tag with the Landon boys while their mothers tried in vain to calm them down. Grace's friends, Anna, Katelyn, and Mary, stood talking.

After not succeeding in escorting Grace to the dance, Thomas had invited another girl named Sarah, and she had accepted the offer. Thomas was standing only a little ways from Sarah, talking to Mary's date, Andrew Brand. Anna and Katelyn on the other hand were content just coming for the food and conversation.

"Hi there!" Grace exclaimed to the girls.

She walked over to her friends and greeted them with hugs. Everyone exchanged hellos, and Katelyn and Mary went to grab some desserts while Grace engaged in a conversation with Anna.

"How have you been?" Grace asked.

"Good. Ethan's birthday was a few days ago, and my

cousins came to visit. Things were a little busy, so I'm glad everything's back to normal."

"I know how that feels," Grace responded.

Just then, Grant came over.

"Hi, Grace!" Grace was one of Grant's favorite people.

"Hi, buddy!" Grace picked up Grant. She looked at him closely and saw cookie crumbs lining his mouth.

"Grant, how about you give Anna one of those delicious cookies that you have in your pocket." Grant gulped. He stared Grace in the eyes for a moment, and then they both burst out laughing.

Soon enough, more families arrived. A little ways from the group, some men started a conversation. Caught up in all the evening's activities, no one even noticed them.

*   *   *

"So what do you think?"

"I agree. He's had his chances. Now he has to pay! It has to be something that will really have an impact on him, something that will make him think about what he's doing."

"The barn. Let's burn the barn."

"When?"

"Tonight during the dance."

*   *   *

Grace and David grabbed their food and sat down with their friends. They all had a merry time, talking, eating, and laughing.

After the meal ended, the fiddles began to play and the dancing began. Grace loved to dance. Every now and again, she would spot Anna and Katelyn standing off to the side, just smiling and clapping their hands to the music. Amid all the dancing and conversation, no one noticed that two of the men had disappeared.

*   *   *

Once the dancing had subsided a little, David and Grace walked away from all the commotion. David suddenly remembered something exciting that he wanted to show Grace.

"Would you mind riding back to my cabin with me quickly? There's something I want to show you," he asked.

"Sure," Grace replied.

David tenderly helped Grace into the wagon. The sunset was beautiful, filling the sky with rays of crimson, auburn, gold, and pink. They were engaged in a nice conversation when suddenly, David pulled the horses to a halt, startling Grace.

"Why did you…" Grace's question was quickly answered when she looked towards the Carvers' farm down below them.

"Come on!" David wildly whipped the reigns, and the horses bolted down the hill. The Carvers' barn was engulfed in flames!

David jumped out of the wagon and ran towards the barn.

"David! It's too late! You can't save it now!" Grace shouted.

"It's not the barn I'm trying to save! Help me!" David quickly grabbed a ladder. He leaned it up against the side of the barn and climbed up to an opening into the hayloft. The flames were spreading rapidly. There was no way to save the animals down below. David quickly moved aside some hay bales. Behind them sat a young Negro boy, frozen in terror.

David grabbed his arm, dragging him towards the window.

"Come on, Solomon!" he yelled.

They both scurried down the ladder just as the hayloft was overcome in a fiery blaze. Grace was at the bottom, waiting for David to come down. She looked up and gasped when she spotted the small fugitive. Once they were both safely on the ground, David looked at the burning barn in horror. Thinking about the helpless animals inside and what it would mean for his family if they lost them, he ran to the well and started to fill the bucket.

"David! No! You can't do anything about it!" Grace shouted, holding him back as he started to run towards the burning barn.

Tears streamed from David's eyes as he watched the barn and everything in it smolder. Grace grabbed the bucket from his hands and pulled him away from the fire.

As David turned away from the burning barn, he spotted something nailed to the side of the house. He grabbed it and read it aloud to Grace.

Carver,

Let this be a warning to you and your family. You'd better stop now or something even worse will happen to you!

At the bottom of the note were the words, "Down with the Negros!" David quickly shoved the paper in his pocket.

David looked at Solomon and instructed him to go inside and stay in his room until they got back. Grace and David then ran to the wagon. The horses were spooked and frenzied. David quickly calmed them, and he and Grace rode back to the dance. David hollered at the team to go faster as his heart raced wildly with panic.

CHAPTER 5

FUGITIVE

As they rode back over the hill, David and Grace noticed that the dance was winding down. Everyone was starting to clean up when David jumped out of the wagon and ran to his parents.

"Father!" he shouted.

"What is it, David?" Mr. Carver asked.

"Someone set the barn on fire!" David exclaimed, trying to catch his breath.

"What?"

"We don't know who it was."

Mr. Carver's eyes were wide, and his heart was beating rapidly. He ran away from the group toward the wagon.

"David!" he yelled. "You and your mother meet me back at the cabin!" He was out of sight in an instant.

Everyone present was in shock. Some got on their horses or in their wagons and rode straight to the Carvers' house to see if they could help.

David put his arm around his mother.

"David!" Grace exclaimed. "You both can ride with us."

David nodded his thanks and hurriedly helped his mother into the wagon beside Grace. Mrs. Johnson and Rebekah ran over and hopped in. Mrs. Johnson turned back to her husband and said sternly yet respectfully, "I'm going whether you approve or not, Tom."

He frowned and then turned away to go back to the cabin.

Upon arriving at the horrible scene, Mr. Carver stared in

disbelief as he watched the nightmare unfolding before his eyes. The others soon joined him.

"Grab the buckets! Fill em' with water! Come on!" Mr. Carver shouted as he dashed to the well with some others.

"Father, no!" David screamed as he grabbed his father's arm, holding him back from running towards the fiery blaze. Mr. Carver stopped trying to escape his son's grasp. The barn was fully engulfed in flames. Children hid their faces in their mothers' skirts as they wept. Wives held onto their husbands, their hearts aching over the terrible fate that had befallen the Carvers.

Everyone stood a safe distance away from the burning barn. Nothing could be done. All was lost.

How could this happen?

"I'm so sorry, Timothy. If I can help in any way–" Mr. Jones, Anna's father, offered as he stood next to Mr. Carver.

"Thank you, Richard, but I'm afraid nothing can be done now."

Mrs. Johnson approached Mrs. Carver, her face downcast.

"Rachel," she quietly said.

"Oh, Clara!" Mrs. Carver burst into tears and embraced Mrs. Johnson.

"I'm so sorry, Rachel."

David stood next to his father, watching the roaring flames. Mr. Carver suddenly remembered Solomon. In code, he worriedly asked David, "My package?"

David replied, "It's safe."

Mr. Carver nodded and whispered a quiet, "Thank God."

Suddenly, tears started to flow uncontrollably as he thought of what this loss would mean for his family.

"How could this have happened?" Mr. Carver asked himself. "I don't understand."

David remembered the note he had found nailed to their house. He pulled it out of his pocket.

"Father," he said, handing him the note, "I found this nailed to the cabin."

Mr. Carver took the note from his son and read it. Its words made his heart heavy.

"God help us," he pleaded.

Grace put her hand on David.

"David, I'm so sorry," she sympathized.

Everyone stared at the terrible sight for a while. News quickly got around that the barn burning wasn't an accident. People were furious.

Everyone took turns consoling the Carvers and offering to help in any way possible. After an hour, everyone had gone home, everyone except the Johnsons.

"Grace," Mrs. Johnson quietly called, "come on, dear."

"Please, Ma. Let me stay a little longer," Grace pleaded, just wanting to be by David's side.

"Alright."

She and Rebekah hugged Mrs. Carver one last time and then rode away.

After everyone was gone, Grace and the Carvers all went inside to see Solomon. Finding him hiding under David's bed, Mr. Carver knelt down, beckoning, "It's alright, Solomon. You can come out now."

Solomon started to come out from under the bed, but he noticed Grace and stopped, wondering who she was and if she were a friend.

"Don't be scared, son. She's a friend," Mr. Carver comforted.

Solomon didn't take his glance off Grace as he slowly came out and seated himself up against the wall.

Suddenly, David became angry at him. What he had gone through earlier plagued his thoughts.

"Solomon, what were you thinking? Why didn't you get out when you saw the flames?" David, half shouting, questioned the frightened boy.

"David," his mother gently rebuked.

"Well, he almost cost us both our lives!"

"I…I'm sorry. I was asleep. Didn't wake up 'til I felt the warmth of the fire 'neath me. By that time, they were 'blazin', and I…I was 'fraid. I just froze. Didn't even think of the window. I was too 'fraid, and the hay was blockin,' so I couldn't see. I…I'm sorry," the boy stuttered.

David lowered his head, regretting how harshly he had spoken.

"It's alright, Solomon," he apologized.

"Come out to the kitchen, Solomon. We'll get you something to eat," Mrs. Carver told him.

Mrs. Carver wrapped her arm around him, and they walked out to the kitchen. Mr. Carver, David, and Grace followed.

Once Solomon had his food, Mrs. Carver sat down at the kitchen table, starting to cry again. Their entire living was in that barn. Grace sat down beside her, gently rubbing her back.

Mr. Carver watched from the kitchen window as the barn and everything in it continued to burn.

"I feel so helpless just watching it burn like this," he said.

They were all silent for a long while. David just kept pacing back and forth across the kitchen floor. Then, suddenly, he burst out, "Who could do something like this?"

Grace and Mrs. Carver looked up at him, startled, and Solomon stopped eating. Mr. Carver, still focusing his glance on the flames, said, "Angry people do bad things, David."

"Whoever did this tonight was evil. I hate them!"

Mr. Carver quickly turned his head to look at his son.

"'Amazing Grace!-how sweet the sound-that saved a wretch like me! I once was lost but now am found, was blind, but now I see.'" He paused then stared hard into his son's eyes. "We're all in need of a Savior, David. Whoever did this tonight is no more wretched than we are."

David stormed out of the house through the back door so that he could no longer see the horrible sight. Grace followed.

"Are you alright?" she gently asked.

"No," he curtly responded. He quickly caught his tone and confessed, "I'm sorry."

"It's alright. I understand."

There was a slight pause in the conversation, and then Grace spoke.

"I'm terribly sorry for you all."

David let out a frustrated scoff and shook his head.

Grace looked at David's downcast face. He didn't look like the strong young man that she knew. He looked weary and troubled.

"About Solomon...you're hiding runaway slav–" Grace started.

"No, he's the only one," David cut her off. "Grace, you must promise to keep this a secret. You can't tell anyone."

"I promise, David. But why is he here?"

"He ran away from a plantation in South Carolina. He said his master beat him so bad he could hardly walk. He was traveling for days, hiding in the woods during the day and running at night. It amazes me how he was able to get this far without getting caught."

"Maybe his absence wasn't noticed because he's so young."

"Not likely. Those slave owners have eagle's eyes. They know when one of their slaves has escaped." David solemnly continued, "What I know for certain, though, is that only the grace of God could have brought him this far."

"How did you find him?"

"My father found him asleep in our fields. He saw his blood-stained shirt and knew he needed help, so he brought him back here. My mother's been tending to his wounds, and they're almost healed. They were pretty bad. We hadn't planned on any visitors, not slaves anyway, so he's been hiding out in the barn. That is until…" David turned his head away from Grace as a single tear rolled down his cheek.

Grace placed her arm around him, and after a moment, asked, "How long has he been here?"

"Four days. His father was separated from him and his mother when they were sold at a slave auction years back, and his mother died just a few months ago from a heart attack. Solomon said she worked all day and sometimes all night. Their master would abuse her and beat her if she did the slightest thing wrong."

"That's terrible."

"I know."

"How old is he?"

"We don't know for sure. My guess is he's no older than nine."

A shiver ran down Grace's spine as she spoke her next words.

"Do you think whoever burned the barn tonight knew he was here?"

"I don't think so," David quietly responded. "Whoever set our barn on fire tonight wouldn't have given up the reward offered for Solomon's capture." David paused for a slight moment then continued. "My father's helping him get to freedom. Some friends of ours have been helping slaves escape since before the war. We're taking him to their house tomorrow night."

"I hope he makes it," Grace said hopefully.

David looked down in regret.

"That boy has been through more than we know. I just had to be a fool and go and yell at him like I did."

"David, don't be so hard on yourself. You've been through a lot tonight."

"I still shouldn't have done it." A righteous anger suddenly overcame him.

He exclaimed, "They should be able to have the same rights we do, and they can't! Why? Because the color of their skin isn't the same as ours!"

"I know, David. It's not fair."

"It's more than 'not fair'; it's cruel!" He stopped for a moment as he choked on his next words. "Losing our barn and our animals is hard, probably the hardest thing that I've ever had to go through." He turned and looked Grace straight in the eyes. "But their worth does not even come close to the worth of human life."

Grace smiled faintly. "I agree, David." She placed her hand on his shoulder. "I'm proud of you and your family."

Suddenly, Mr. Carver came out of the house.

"You two might want to see this," he whispered to David and Grace. They looked at each other and followed him into the house. Mr. Carver motioned for them to be quiet. Sitting up against the wall in David's room, Solomon was covered with a blanket, quietly singing to himself.

David and Grace listened, trying to catch all the words.

"Oh, beautiful freedom,
I long for thee!
Your majesty shines,
From sea to sea.

And, oh, that someday,
I may see it bright and clear.
Then, I would fully know,
That joy that's so dear.

Oh, reign my dear freedom,
For all of my days.
I'll sing 'cross the land,
Of your glory and grace!

I pray for that peace,
That only you bring.
Shine forth like the stars,
Oh, my freedom, please ring."

Grace walked over to Solomon when he had finished.

"That was a nice song you were singing," she told him.

Solomon was startled. He didn't know he had an audience.

Grace continued, "May I ask what song it was?"

"My mother taught it to me. It tells o' the freedom we want so badly." He looked up at Grace. "The freedom you whites have."

*   *   *

Back at home, Grace entered the kitchen where her mother and father were quietly sitting at the table, drinking their coffee. Rebekah was in bed.

"Grace!" Mrs. Johnson exclaimed as she rose to meet her daughter. Mr. Johnson put his coffee cup down and went into his bedroom, closing the door behind him.

Grace looked away from her mother as she mumbled her next words.

"Their barn's gone. It's nothing more than a heap of ashes now. Oh, Ma, they lost everything!" Grace burst into tears.

Mrs. Johnson wrapped her arms around Grace.

"We need to keep the Carvers in our prayers. They've been such a blessing to so many of us."

"But how could anyone be so heartless? The Carvers never did anything wrong to anyone, and this is what they get for trying to help the Negros. It's not right!"

Mrs. Johnson took Grace's face in her hands and looked her in the eyes.

"The Carvers didn't deserve to have their barn burned, but it was. Jesus didn't deserve to die, but He did. And why did He? To fulfill God's plan. We need to trust in the Lord, Grace. We don't know why He's allowing this to happen, but

He knows better than we do."

Grace continued to weep, and Mrs. Johnson stood for a long time, embracing her broken daughter.

After a time, she finally spoke.

"Now, you should really get to bed. You'll feel better in the morning." Grace nodded obediently and then walked into her room, closing the door behind her. She fell down on her bed in dismay.

"Why God? Why?" She exclaimed and fell asleep sobbing.

CHAPTER 6

A SORROWFUL DEPARTURE

Two days passed. Grace got out of bed each morning, exhausted from her lack of sleep. Her face was downcast, and her eyes were swollen red from all the tears she had shed.

On the third morning, Mrs. Johnson walked in with a tea cup in her hand, smiling at Grace. She handed it to Grace and sat down on the bed beside her.

"Why don't you come into town with me, today? It might help take your mind off of things."

Grace nodded in reply.

*   *   *

In town Mrs. Johnson and Grace were walking through the mercantile when they ran into Mrs. Carver.

"Hello, Rachel," Mrs. Johnson greeted Mrs. Carver.

"Hello, Clara," she replied sadly. "Hello, Grace. I'm glad I ran into you. I was hoping to be able to tell you the news in person. You see…we're moving away."

"What?" Mrs. Johnson asked. She looked at Grace, who stood silent in shock.

"My father and mother live in Kentucky. A few weeks ago, we received a letter from my father saying that he wanted us to move back with him. Apparently, he's been having a lot of trouble managing the farm, and his hired hand is getting married. Timothy didn't want to move away because he didn't want to leave the church. He felt it would be abandoning God's work and his flock. Just last week, though, we received another letter from my mother saying that my father had had a stroke.

He's confined to his bed. His whole left side is paralyzed. Now there's no one to run the farm, and with our barn and animals now gone, we have no way to make a living. We can't afford to buy new animals. So we're moving to Kentucky to live with my parents. Lord willing we'll be coming back in the future. After all, our friends are here, and Timothy couldn't bear the thought of parting with his church forever. For now, though, he's made arrangements for our friend Kevin Smith to fill in for him while we're gone."

"How long do you plan on staying away?" Mrs. Johnson asked.

"We don't know for sure, but it looks like a year at the least. With Father being in this kind of condition, we're going to have to manage the farm."

Up until this point, Grace had stood silently, but a hundred thoughts were racing through her mind. *This means David's going to have to leave, too,* she thought.

"Mrs. Carver, David wouldn't happen to be in town, would he?" Grace questioned.

"No, he isn't, Grace. He's at home packing some things up for our trip. We plan to leave as soon as possible."

"I hope Timothy is preaching tomorrow?" Mrs. Johnson asked.

"Yes, he is. Tomorrow will be his last sermon. We're going to say all our goodbyes afterwards."

"Is there any way we can help you, Rachel?"

"No, but thank you, Clara."

"We'll keep on praying for you all."

"Thank you. I'll see you tomorrow at church?"

"We'll be there."

Mrs. Johnson and Grace walked out of the mercantile. They got in the wagon and drove home.

"They're moving?" Grace asked herself, not wanting to believe that everything she had just heard was a reality. "Oh, Ma!"

"I know, Grace," Mrs. Johnson sadly responded.

"David shouldn't have to go. He's old enough to make his own decisions."

"David is going to have to help his father with the farm, Grace. You know that. Family comes first."

"But…" Grace sighed then admitted, "You're right. Mr. Carver won't be able to run the farm all by himself. But that doesn't make me feel any better."

"Now, now. It'll be alright. After all, Mrs. Carver said they plan on coming back, and maybe then things will have calmed down, and you and David can get married."

"I hope so, Ma. I want it so badly! I hope David wants it as much as I do."

"You know he does, Grace."

"It seems so strange knowing that tomorrow will be the last time David and I see each other, for years maybe."

*   *   *

The sermon the next morning was a sad one. Reverend Carver filled it with wonderful memories that the congregation had shared together, his sorrow at the thought of leaving them, and the faith that God would be with them all wherever they went in life. Grace was hardly listening. Instead, she was staring at David, who was seated two pews in front of her. She was reminiscing about all the great times they had had. Grace couldn't help but wonder if all of her dreams about their life together were now being shattered.

Afterwards, everyone came up to Reverend and Mrs. Carver to say goodbye and wish them God's blessings. Grace approached David slowly, her heart aching.

"Hello, David."

"Hello, Grace." David paused for a slight moment and then continued. "Would you like to take a walk?"

Grace nodded, and they went outside. They stood under the grand oak tree, Grace leaning up against its trunk with her back towards David. She couldn't bring herself to look into his eyes, knowing that this could be the last time she ever saw him.

"You know I don't want to leave, Grace." David's heart was torn. "I've been dreaming of the life we could share together, just as you have. But Father will need my help running the farm. I promise, though, that not a day will pass when I don't miss you. I might be moving away, but my love is staying with you."

Grace could no longer hold her emotions back. She turned towards David as the tears flowed freely down her cheeks.

"I love you, David Carver. Promise you'll come back to me!"

He came closer to her and held her trembling hands in his own.

"I promise."

"I'll hold you to that. You know I will."

"Yes, I know you, Grace Johnson. When someone says they'll do something, you hold them to it, and I love you for that. I love everything about you. And I will come back. I hope that your father will let me take your hand in marriage when I do. By then, you'll be of age."

"I don't think it's the age that bothers him. I think it's the fact that your family are such strong believers. He hates that, you know."

"It's that bad, then?"

"Yes. I've been praying for years that he'll get saved, but God doesn't seem to be listening."

"He's always listening, Grace. Sometimes He just doesn't answer our prayers the way we'd like Him to. But He knows what's best. We just have to–"

"Trust Him." Grace finished his sentence.

"That's right."

There was a pause, and then David continued.

"I will write you as often as I can. And I want *you* to promise me that you'll write back."

Grace was able to give a small laugh and then replied, "I promise."

She hugged David, and he gently wiped away her tears.

"I love you," he softly told her.

"I love you, too."

As David turned and walked back towards the church, Grace blew a kiss after him.

"I will miss you more than you know," she whispered.

And so, another beautiful yet sorrowful memory was made beneath the mighty arms of the oak tree.

CHAPTER 7

BROKENHEARTED

After Mrs. Johnson had said her goodbyes, she approached Grace, who sat leaning up against the oak tree's strong trunk, weeping.

"Grace," she said softly, sitting down beside her heartbroken daughter.

"This is horrible!"

"He'll come back for you."

Mrs. Johnson sat next to Grace, consoling her for quite some time.

"This war has caused a lot of pain and suffering for many people, not just us, Grace. Think of all those brave men who have died. We need to be brave, too, and just keep trusting the Lord. It's already been several months since the war started. I think it will end soon."

"Do you really think so, Ma?"

"I do," Mrs. Johnson reassured her troubled daughter.

Mrs. Johnson gazed into Grace's tearful eyes. In reality, she had no idea how long the war would last. But right now, she was only concerned about comforting her hurting daughter.

"I'll miss him so much!" Grace cried.

"I know you will, but he'll be back. And I hope then that the war will be over and your father's heart will be changed towards the Carvers."

"Do you honestly think that Father will change? That David and I will be able to marry?"

"Of course I do. But for the time being, you must think

about the Carvers' safety. With all the tension right now, moving away is probably the best thing for them."

Grace nodded. She felt better knowing that David would be moving away to a safer environment.

"Now come on. Let's go home." Mrs. Johnson gently took hold of Grace's hand and helped her to her feet.

CHAPTER 8

SCARLET FEVER

It was now February of 1865, and Grace was nineteen years old. Three and a half years had passed since the Carvers had moved away. They had been away longer than they had expected. A few small things had happened at the Johnson farm over the past few years but nothing of any great significance. Their life was a quiet one. Much of Grace's time was spent at home. She waited fervently for David's return.

Mrs. Johnson had received letters almost every other month from Mrs. Carver since their departure. Grace also had received dozens from David. Now, in February another letter arrived.

"Ma! Ma! It's a letter from Mrs. Carver!" Grace exclaimed as she ran out of the post office and towards Mrs. Johnson.

"Grace, quiet down. It's not ladylike to shout," Mrs. Johnson gently rebuked.

"I'm sorry. I'm just so excited!"

"Well, get into the wagon, and we can read it on the way."

On the way home Grace read the letter to her mother. Not all the news was pleasant. Mrs. Carver's father had died, and her mother was in a poor condition without her husband. The doctor said he did not expect her to live much longer, either.

"Poor Rachel," Mrs. Johnson mourned.

Grace continued reading the letter.

Timothy is planning on selling the farm. He says he's been away from his church far too long and wishes to return home to Virginia hopefully sometime in May. The Lord has been good to us. We have new, strong animals to return home with, more than we had before. Mother is going to accompany us. We were concerned about her making the trip, but she assures us that she will be fine and that a change will be good for her. However, I'm worried. At times she is so downcast that she exclaims how desperately she longs to die so she can be with my father again. I wish she wouldn't speak that way because it distresses me to think of her absence.

I included a letter for Grace from David. He speaks of her every day. My love to your family.

Rachel

My dear Grace,

I think of you every day. I dream about the life I hope we can share together when I return. Sometimes I speak aloud of it to my parents. They are both almost as fond of you as I am. I love you dearly. I have continued to pray for your family and that your father will give me your hand in marriage when I return. I'm so glad that we are finally coming back! I don't think I could live another month without seeing your beautiful face.

Truly and forever yours,
David

"They're coming home!" Grace jubilantly proclaimed.

"That's such great news," Mrs. Johnson rejoiced.

"I'll put the letter with the others."

"Make sure your father doesn't see it. It's never my intention to keep secrets from him, but in this instance, I think it's permissible."

"Of course it is," Grace reassured her.

Rebekah rode in the back of the wagon the whole ride home without saying a word. She was burning. Her throat was dry. She felt like fainting. However, the two women didn't even remember she was there, being so caught up in the excitement of the letter.

When they arrived home, Grace hurried into her bedroom. Shutting the door behind her, she held the letter tight to her chest. She couldn't wait for David to come home! Three and a half years was too long for them to have been apart.

Suddenly, there was a thud outside Grace's door. Mrs. Johnson, startled by the loud noise, quickly turned around to find Rebekah lying on the floor, unconscious.

"Tom! Tom, come quickly!" she cried.

Mr. Johnson ran over to his wife. Picking up Rebekah, they both laid her on her bed. Startled by her mother's yelling, Grace had left her room and was now standing beside her parents. Mrs. Johnson reached down and felt Rebekah's flushed face.

"She's as hot as fire! Tom, go fetch Doctor Hays, quickly!"

"Ma, I'll go!" Grace answered anxiously. She ran out the door, saddled up Violet, and took off. The winter wind brushed up against her face as she pressed Violet to hurry on.

Upon entering town, she halted Violet in front of Dr.

Hays's office, jumped down, and darted inside.

Bursting into the office, she cried, almost out of breath, "Doctor Hays! You...you have to come quickly! It's Rebekah! She collapsed, and she's burning up!"

Doctor Hays quickly grabbed his coat, gloves, and medical kit and hurried out the door with Grace.

Once they arrived at the Johnsons' cabin, they both tied up their horses and rushed into the house. Doctor Hays bent down beside Rebekah and felt her forehead. She was slipping in and out of consciousness.

"It's scarlet fever," Doctor Hays sorrowfully announced. "Where has Rebekah been besides here?"

"Well, yesterday she was over at the Aldens," Mrs. Johnson replied nervously.

"That's probably where she picked it up. It's going around right now. I'll have to ride over to their place after I'm done here. Grace, fetch me some towels and cool water!" He rolled up his sleeves and knelt down beside Rebekah. "I can't bleed her. She's just too weak. She'd die if I did. We have to try to bring the fever down the best we can; otherwise, her chances of survival are slim."

"But we've all had the fever, and we recovered," Mrs. Johnson protested.

"Rebekah's system is much weaker than the rest of yours. Some people, especially children, don't take sicknesses as well as others do, and scarlet fever's the worst of all."

Grace returned with the towels and some water.

"Thank you, Grace. It's important that we change these every ten minutes or so." He placed a soaking towel on Rebekah's feverish head. "Clara and Grace, I want you to grab

Rebekah's things and take them outside. Tom, you'd better go out with them to help get a fire going. We have to burn all of Rebekah's things, everything she's touched. Blankets, clothing—everything."

Grace stared at her sister. Rebekah's cheeks were scarlet red. Her entire body was soaked with sweat. Her temperature was rising by the minute. Grace wondered if her sister would be able to pull through as the rest of them had. She hoped beyond all reason that her dear sister would survive. Her heart told her one thing, but reason told her another. But wasn't God above reason? Didn't He have the power to save Rebekah? To perform a miracle?

Grabbing a few of Rebekah's things, including her doll, Hannah, Grace left the room. Mr. Johnson lit a fire, and Grace watched as all of Rebekah's dearest items disappeared in the fiery blaze: the knitted blanket that Grace had watched her mother tediously labor over for weeks to welcome Rebekah into the world; Hannah, who had never left Rebekah's side since she had received her for her third birthday; and the sweater that Grace had made for Rebecca to keep her warm when she was ill. Grace's heart shattered into a million pieces. She had watched the Carvers' barn burn three and a half years ago, and now she watched as her sister's precious possessions burned as well. For the first time, Grace thought about the extent of the damage one spark could cause. That spark could burn precious possessions, but it could not burn the memories; it could scorch them, but it couldn't destroy them.

Re-entering the house, they all hurried back into Rebekah's room. Doctor Hays gave them directions and quickly left for the Aldens, promising that he would return as soon as possible.

Night came on suddenly, enveloping the tiny cabin and its inhabitants in complete darkness. A single candle flickered by Rebekah's bedside. It provided just enough light for the family to assist her and still allow her to get some precious hours of sleep. All three of them had a restless night, changing the towels that were soaked with Rebekah's sweat. Mrs. Johnson urged Rebekah to try to drink some water, but it was nearly impossible for the ailing girl.

By morning, they were all exhausted. Then, just as it felt as if they had no strength left in them, they all heard the sound that they dreaded the most: a cough, then another cough, followed by another and another. They all looked at each other with worried expressions. Everyone was silent.

"It's the last stage of it, Tom! Doctor Hays warned us. If she continues, she'll suffocate!" Mrs. Johnson exclaimed nervously.

"Go fetch Doctor Hays, Grace, quickly!" she commanded.

Grace obeyed and ran out of the house. The morning air was cold and bit her face as she rode the long distance to the Aldens. She knocked on the door, and when she did not get an immediate answer, she burst into the house.

"Doctor Hays–" she stopped mid-sentence. Before her eyes was a horrible sight: Mrs. Alden was on the ground, weeping and grasping her husband, who sat beside her. Doctor Hays slowly covered the faces of the three Alden children, who lay lifeless on their beds. The fever had taken them all.

Doctor Hays, surprised at Grace's sudden arrival, looked at her, but Grace seemed to have forgotten what she was going to say. The horror she was witnessing was too much.

She thought of her dying sister and how high her chances of survival could truly be.

"Doctor Hays," she stammered, "it's Rebekah. The coughing has started, and it won't stop."

Doctor Hays readied his things. Before exiting, he bent down near Mr. and Mrs. Alden. "I'm so sorry. I did all I could."

"We know. Thank you, Doc," Mr. Alden said between tears. Then, he turned his glance towards Grace. "I pray that this cursed fever won't take Rebekah, too."

Grace felt her heart beating wildly. She felt like fainting.

Grace and Doctor Hays arrived back at the Johnsons' cabin, but it was too late. They walked in just in time to hear Mrs. Johnson burst into tears.

"No! No! Why God? Why? Oh, Tom!" Mrs. Johnson yelled and wept hysterically. Trembling, she collapsed onto the floor.

Grace ran over to her parents, and Mr. Johnson wrapped his strong arms around them both. He tried to be strong for his wife and daughter, but his heart was broken.

Doctor Hays placed his hand on Mr. Johnson's shoulder and whispered, "I'm so sorry."

Mr. Johnson could not bring himself to say anything, and Doctor Hays quietly and solemnly left the house.

Grace felt like the whole world had just come to an end. Her dear sister–her only sister–was gone. How could she live without her? How foolish she had been not to have spent more time with her. How she regretted it! And now, she could never get those times back. They were gone forever.

* * *

The funeral was a quiet one, consisting only of family

and close friends. Rebekah was buried outside under her favorite tree, a cherry tree. On bright summer days Rebekah had sat beneath it while the blossoms gently fell all around her. Leaning against its trunk, she would write about her memories and her hopes for the future, and she would draw the beautiful scenes that surrounded her: the bright, blue sky with fluffy, white clouds and the occasional animals that she would spot crawling or leaping through the tall grass. She had been a quiet child, and even though weak and often prone to sickness, she had been content with the peaceful life she had lived. When Rebekah used to sit beneath her cherry tree, she would marvel at her blessings and God's beauty that was all around her.

As Grace now stood at this spot, looking down at her lonely sister's grave, a sense of grief came over her that she had never known before. She realized now that all the times she had spent with her sister—playing tag on a family picnic, sitting beside her in the pew at church, making her birthday cake and snuggling with her beside the fire on a cold winter evening—were the memories she now treasured the most. She pondered all the times she had spent with David while Rebekah had sat alone in her room, sick and lonesome. Grace wished she had spent more time with her dearest sister, who now lay buried beneath her in the earth. She wished that she could have erased all the bad memories Rebekah had had of her from her mind. She wondered what Rebekah's last thoughts were before she died. Had she been mad at Grace for all the times that Grace had left her to go and be with David? Did she wish that she could have lived a healthy, joyful life like Grace? If only Rebekah could have been there to answer these questions that haunted Grace's mind! For she would have replied with a simple no to them all. These were not the thoughts Rebekah had had on her deathbed.

Rebekah had loved her sister more than she had loved anyone else. She had looked up to Grace. There was a special bond that she had felt towards her sister that she could not have described, a bond that all sisters should feel for one another. And yet, Rebekah had known that Grace was growing up and that her mind had started to shift from family affairs to other things outside the home. She had known that Grace would marry someday, and she had prayed that Grace and David would someday be together. Even though she had been weak and sick almost her entire childhood, she had not despised her life. She had known that her Savior had called her home and that He was doing it out of love, not cruelty. And so the last thoughts Rebekah had had on her deathbed were not of sorrow but of joy; not of anger but of love; not of a longing for the life she was losing but of the life she prayed her sister would find.

CHAPTER 9

EVIL OR KINDNESS?

After the funeral, Mr. and Mrs. Johnson went back inside. They sat at the kitchen table in complete silence for almost an hour. Finally, Mr. Johnson spoke, but it was not the love and comfort that his wife was longing to hear.

"Why would the loving God that you believe in allow this to happen?" he angrily questioned his wife, rising from his seat and walking to the window.

"He knows better than we do, Tom. He never does anything to hurt us," Mrs. Johnson replied through tears. Mr. Johnson threw his head back mockingly and rolled his eyes.

"No! He took our Rebekah from us. Rebekah was the sweetest girl who ever lived. She never did anything wrong! Taking her was just plain evil, that's what it was! Plain evil!"

"God isn't capable of doing evil, Tom. Evil entered the world through sin, through our sin. We brought it upon ourselves. God *is* good! He *is* love! He didn't *take* our Rebekah from us; He *received* her! The life she would have had here would have been bad for her. She was weak, and she had always been. He received her into His kingdom."

A slight smile crossed Mrs. Johnson's face as she thought of where her precious daughter now was.

"She's not sick anymore. She feels no more pain. He was helping her when He let her go. He spared her from all the pain and sickness she would have had here in the future!"

Mrs. Johnson paused a moment, wiping the tears from her eyes. She looked back up at her husband.

"Of course we wanted her to stay, but that wouldn't have been best for her. I think it would have been harder for us to have watched her suffer, knowing that she would never get well, than it was to let her go. The Lord did us all a great kindness!" She choked back her tears and cried, "Even though it hurts right now, I know that He did what was best for all of us."

Mr. Johnson slowly walked back to the table and took his wife's hands in his.

"I'm sorry, Clara. I shouldn't have been so harsh. Forgive me?" He brought her hands up to his lips and tenderly kissed them.

Mrs. Johnson nodded in response.

Grace had been listening to the conversation through her bedroom door and now returned to her bed where she had been reading Revelation 21:4 just a few minutes before: "And God shall wipe away every tear from their eyes; and there shall be no more death, neither mourning, nor crying, neither shall there be any more pain, for the old order of things has passed away."

Grace pondered these words. It was a great comfort to her knowing where Rebekah was; she was with her Savior. She was in no more pain; she shed no more tears. And Grace knew that someday she, too, would get to live in that wonderful place that God had prepared for her, a place where she would mourn over her sister's death no more, but would see her face to face once again. What blessed assurance!

Grace knew that even though she was hurting, God hadn't abandoned her. He had promised to be right there beside her, comforting and loving her every step of the way. She knew that whatever trials she came across in life were tools that her loving God used to teach and mold her to become more like Himself. He wasn't doing it out of cruelty; He was doing it out of love, all for His glory and all for her good.

"Lord, you know I'm suffering. Please give me Your grace and Your strength to go on," she quietly prayed.

She held her Bible close, leaned back on her pillow, and fell asleep.

*   *   *

One month rolled by. Every morning, the pattern was the same: Grace would walk into the kitchen to find her father sitting in complete silence, frozen in his seat. He didn't move. He didn't smile. He didn't say a word. His face was downcast. His cup of coffee sat in front of him on the table, untouched.

Mrs. Johnson wasn't much better. She would smile faintly as Grace entered the kitchen. Pouring herself some tea, Mrs. Johnson would seat herself across from her husband. This pattern continued until one morning late March.

Grace came out of her room. Mrs. Johnson poured herself some tea, and together they sat down at the table across from Mr. Johnson. This morning, however, instead of the normal silence from Mr. Johnson, he suddenly burst into tears. Over the past month, he had tried his best to hide his emotions, crying only when he was alone. But now, he couldn't hide it anymore. The pain was too great.

Mrs. Johnson looked at her husband's tear-stained face. In all the years they had been married, she had never seen him cry before. Now the tears came nonstop. She desperately wished that he would turn to the Savior's grace, which was so freely offered. She hoped that God would use this horrible trial to draw her husband unto Himself and make him realize how much he needed Him. Similar thoughts ran through Grace's mind, too.

When Mr. Johnson's weeping finally subsided, Grace pushed back from the table and quietly told her mother, "I'm gonna go out to the barn."

Mrs. Johnson looked up and nodded gently. Quietly, Grace put on her coat, hat, and gloves and went outside. It was a crisp winter day. The sun was peeking through the clouds, and there was only a dusting of snow on the ground. Grace was greatly looking forward to spring's arrival. The gloom of winter brought everyone's spirits down. She entered the barn and looked around her. Suddenly, the scene of the Carvers' barn burning down came to mind. How sorry she felt for them. She was extremely thankful that they had moved away for a while. She prayed that no further harm would come to them when they returned.

All of a sudden, a strange feeling came over her. Grace couldn't explain why, but she desperately wanted to go and visit the Carvers' place. So that's exactly what she did.

Upon arriving at the abandoned farm, she tied Violet to the half-broken fence post and walked around. The house looked the same from the outside, but when she entered, it was not so. Things had drastically changed. Cobwebs hung everywhere, and she spotted a few rats occasionally scurrying near her feet. The wooden furniture stood in the same place. The Carvers had left it, knowing that it would be of no use to them in Kentucky. They had, however, taken everything else: the dishes, bed spreads, and rugs were all gone. The house looked forgotten.

An idea suddenly popped into Grace's head.

If the Carvers are coming home in the spring, this place should be fixed up for them. I'm sure the men from church would volunteer to build a new barn. After all, Mr. Carver was good friends with Mr. Brendon. I'm sure he'd donate the needed lumber.

With this idea, Grace returned home, her spirits cheered a little. She planned on sharing it with Reverend Smith on Sunday.

CHAPTER 10

REBUILDING AND RENOVATION

On Sunday, Mrs. Johnson and Grace went to church. It was only the third service they had attended since Rebekah's death, and they were still not used to Rebekah's place in the wagon being unoccupied.

Upon arriving, Grace and her mother tied up the horses and went inside. They were a little early, and Reverend Smith was there preparing for the sermon.

"Good morning, ladies. You're early," Reverend Smith greeted them.

"Yes, Reverend. Grace had something she wanted to speak with you about," Mrs. Johnson responded.

"What might that be?" he asked, coming down from the pulpit where he had been organizing his notes.

"Well, Reverend, as you probably know, the Carvers are coming home soon," Grace started.

"Yes, I just got a letter from them a few days ago. I'm looking forward to their return."

"Yes, well, I thought it might be helpful if we…" Grace nervously stopped, knowing that this would be a big task to have the congregation undertake.

"Speak up. It's alright," Reverend Smith gently urged.

"I know it's a lot to ask, but I thought it might be a blessing to the Carvers if we cleaned up their house and rebuilt their barn. After all, Mr. Carver is already going to have a lot of work to do once he gets back, and I thought if men from the congregation were willing to help, we could have it done in no time. And I'm sure that Mr. Brendon would provide the lumber we would need since he's such a good friend of the Carvers."

Reverend Smith stood thinking for a moment.

"That's very thoughtful of you, Grace, but I don't know if Mr. Brendon will go as far as donating all the lumber. I do, however, think the congregation would be willing to make some contributions and that should take care of it. Would you like me to present your request to the congregation?"

"That's actually the reason I came to you first, Reverend."

"I figured that, and I'd be more than happy to."

"Thank you. I'm sure the Carvers will be very appreciative."

"I'm sure they will be."

Just before the sermon, Reverend Smith presented Grace's request. Sadly, the congregation had decreased significantly when the war began. Once Mr. Carver had announced his strong hatred of slavery, many people had left and never returned. But those that were present were more than willing to contribute some money to go towards the rebuilding, and Mr. Brendon said that he would donate as much lumber as possible. The men were excited to help their friend by rebuilding the barn, and they agreed that the following Friday and Saturday would be the perfect days to do it. The women also agreed that they would help clean the house and prepare food for everyone to eat afterwards. Everything was working out just as Grace had hoped it would.

*   *   *

Friday came. The Johnsons ate breakfast, and then Mrs. Johnson told her husband, "Grace and I will be gone today, Tom. We have some things to get done."

Mr. Johnson hesitated for a moment. His mood had changed slightly, but he was still greatly distressed.

"Alright," he consented.

The five families that made up the congregation along with Reverend Smith showed up at the Carvers' to help, including Grace's friends, Anna, Mary, and Katelyn. Two wagons pulled up in front of the house filled with the needed lumber, and the men got to work. Thankfully, there was something for everyone to do.

The women and girls helped out in the house. Some dusted the furniture while some swept and washed the floors. Others cleaned the windows, which were so dirty they could barely see through them anymore.

At lunch time, the table was full of delicious food: fried chicken, potatoes, fruit, and punch. There were even pies and cookies for dessert. The men and boys decided to eat outside while the women and girls ate theirs in the cabin, relaxing in the welcomed shade.

Once they were all finished eating, everyone resumed their work. No one complained or begrudged their tasks. They were doing it for friends and, more importantly, for the Lord. That's all they cared about.

"I'm so glad the house is getting cleaned. I mean, can you imagine if we had left all this work for the Carvers to do? It'd be overwhelming for them," Grace told Anna.

"I know. It's feels good to do the Lord's work and help others," she responded.

The women and girls soon finished the house work. To pass the time, some knitted while the younger girls played with dolls they had brought.

"What are you working on?" Anna questioned Grace.

"It's a blanket. I thought it would make a nice welcome-home gift."

"It's beautiful."

"Mrs. Carver's favorite color is purple, and I thought it would add some nice color to the house."

*   *   *

At home later that evening, the girls found Mr. Johnson seated at the kitchen table, sipping a cup of coffee.

"Did you have a good day, dear?" Mrs. Johnson asked her husband.

"Yes," he responded.

"I'm glad." Mrs. Johnson started to head into her bedroom when Mr. Johnson called out, "Clara, where were you today?"

"We were helping out a neighbor," she replied, trying to act calm.

"Where were you?" he repeated firmly.

Mrs. Johnson's heart started pounding. She could not escape this.

"We were at the Carvers'," she replied nervously.

"What were you doing there?"

She stood silent.

"Answer me, Clara! What were you doing at the Carvers'?"

"We were cleaning."

"Cleaning what?"

"The cabin. We wanted it to be in good shape when they return."

"How could you disobey me like that, Clara?" he shouted.

"We–"

"And you, young lady!" Mr. Johnson turned towards Grace.

"Don't get her involved, Tom! She didn't do anything wrong. We were helping out a neighbor and nothing else."

"'Helping out a neighbor?' When I distinctly told you to have nothing to do with them?"

"The Carvers are good people. Just because everyone doesn't agree with you doesn't mean they're wrong!"

"In this case, they are! The Negros are Negros and nothing else! And if anyone continues to tell you otherwise, I will make sure that you never step foot in that church or any other church again!"

"You can't keep us from going to church, Tom. It's only because of the likes of that John Miller that you believe the way you do! And I think deep down inside, you know that you're wrong."

Mr. Johnson let out a huff, stomped past his wife, and slammed the bedroom door shut. Grace looked at her mother with tears in her eyes.

"We will continue to do what's right, Grace, no matter the cost," Mrs. Johnson declared.

The next morning, Mr. Johnson didn't say a word to his wife or daughter. He walked right past them both and began his work.

"Ma, I don't think we should go to the Carvers' today," Grace quietly warned.

Mrs. Johnson sighed. "I know, Grace. Our work there is finished anyways."

"What will happen when Mr. Carver resumes preaching again?"

"I don't know for sure, Grace, but I do know one thing: Your father will not stop us from going to church. He knew when he married me that I was a Christian, and I'm holding to my beliefs," Mrs. Johnson bravely related.

"Me, too," Grace agreed.

CHAPTER 11

WELCOME HOME!

Another month passed. The barn was rebuilt, and the house was clean, both ready for the Carvers' return. Everyone had worked hard, and it had all paid off.

The Carvers returned on a bright and sunny Saturday afternoon and came right into town to pick up some supplies for their cabin. They did not know about the great surprise that awaited them back at their farm. Grace, also, did not know of the great surprise that awaited her outside the mercantile.

As Grace came down the steps of the mercantile, she heard someone call her name. She looked around. When Grace spotted whom the call had come from, she froze. There stood David, holding his hat in his hands. For a moment they were both too surprised to move. Then, excitement overwhelmed them both.

"Grace!" David exclaimed.

"David!" she shouted back.

David ran towards her as she hurried down the steps of the mercantile. David caught Grace in his arms and spun her around. Then, he gently set her back down, and they hugged one another.

"Oh, it's so good to see you, Grace!"

"And you! David, I can't begin to express all the joy I'm feeling right now!"

"Grace, is that you?" Mrs. Carver questioned as she and Mr. Carver approached.

"Mrs. Carver!" They, too, exchanged hugs.

"How have you been?" Grace asked politely.

"God has been good to us. We're all thankful to be home," Mrs. Carver responded.

"Is your mother with you?" Grace asked innocently.

Mrs. Carver hesitated before answering.

"My mother passed away about a month ago," she solemnly related.

"I'm so sorry," Grace said as her heart suddenly became heavy.

"It comforts me knowing that she's with the Lord," Mrs. Carver said, managing a weak smile.

There was a slight pause and then Grace uttered, "I guess this is an appropriate time to tell you...Rebekah passed away, too."

"Oh, Grace," Mrs. Carver sympathized.

"How?" David asked.

"Scarlet fever. Within a day of detecting it, she was gone."

David tenderly wrapped his arm around Grace's shoulder. After some silence, Mr. Carver spoke, trying to comfort Grace.

"God was watching out for you and your parents, Grace. You could have caught it just as easily, but you didn't."

"I know. He was good to us. We know where she is, and that's a great relief," Grace replied, her spirits having lifted a little. They were all silent for a moment. Then, Grace quickly tried to change the subject.

"I wanted to ask you, did Solomon ever make it to freedom? He's been on my mind lately," Grace asked.

"Yes, he did," Mr. Carver replied. "He's been living with a family in Canada for the past couple of years. Apparently, he's been doing well."

"That's good to hear. I was praying for him," Grace told them.

"Thank you," Mrs. Carver answered.

They stood there talking for a couple of minutes, and then Grace questioned, "So, have you been back home yet?"

"No, we just stopped in to pick up a few things before heading back. Mr. Carver was going to see Mr. Brendon about some lumber for the barn and—" Mrs. Carver stopped.

Grace let out a chuckle. She couldn't help herself. She was so eager to see the look on all of their faces when they discovered their surprise.

"What? Why are you laughing?" Mrs. Carver asked, confused. Mr. Carver and David were also exchanging similar glances of confusion.

"I'm sorry," Grace apologized. "But…oh! You have to come with me!"

"What? Why?" David asked, even more perplexed.

"Just come on!" Grace said enthusiastically, smiling all the while. She could not contain all her excitement.

Grace rode with the Carvers back to their farm. Grace was slightly ahead in her wagon while the Carvers followed close behind. Then, once she got to the top of the hill, she motioned for them to stop. She waved her hand for them to get out of their wagon and come up to her.

"Grace, what are you doing?" David questioned.

"You'll just have to wait and see. Close your eyes!" she instructed, unable to wipe away the huge smile that swept across her face.

The three of them complied.

"Hold hands," she ordered sweetly.

Grace led them to the edge of the hill with the farm down below.

"Open your eyes!"

The Carvers gasped as they beheld the wonderful sight. There stood the new barn even larger than the first one. They were unable to speak for a long while. Their hearts were filled with gratitude. Mr. Carver shook his head in disbelief. The tears slowly flowed from Mrs. Carver's eyes as the thought of someone showing them this much kindness touched her heart. David stood completely still, staring at the barn down below.

"Who?" Mr. Carver and David asked.

"All the men and boys from the congregation!" Grace exclaimed. "And wait till you see the house!"

"The house?" Mrs. Carver asked, amazed that anyone could have blessed them this much.

"Yes. Come on!" Grace urged.

They hopped in their wagons and rode down the hill together. Grace held Mrs. Carver's hand as they entered the house. Although it was rather bare, it was clean. Grace's blanket draped over the rocker added just the right touch. Mrs. Carver was again speechless, so Grace spoke.

"All the women from the congregation did this. They cleaned the windows, dusted, swept, polished the floors, and Anna picked these flowers for you," Grace announced, displaying the vase that had once held beautiful wildflowers. "I'm afraid they're quite wilted by now, though." Grace smiled, and Mrs. Carver chuckled at the dead flowers. She looked around in amazement. Her eyes caught Grace's blanket, and she went over to the rocker and tenderly touched it.

"Who made this?" she asked.

"I did," Grace humbly told her.

"Oh, Grace, it's beautiful! How can we ever thank you?"

"You don't have to. That's what friends are for."

Mrs. Carver wrapped her arms around Grace and squeezed her tight.

"Thank you so much, Grace. You're quite an amazing young woman!" Mr. Carver proclaimed, walking over next to Grace and Mrs. Carver.

"Yes, Grace, you are amazing. I don't know what I'd do without you!" David exclaimed.

CHAPTER 12

PERSECUTION

The following day at church, Reverend Smith gave a brief welcome back speech for the Carvers. Before starting the sermon, Reverend Carver thanked everyone for the great blessing they had given them. This took quite a few minutes, for he did not want to miss the slightest detail. Even after the sermon, the Carvers took the time to approach every family and personally thank them.

The sermon was poignant and timely. Reverend Carver shared all the great things God had done in his family's life since their departure and told the congregation how good it was to be back among them. Then, as with almost all his sermons before he had left, his topic switched to that of the war.

"Before you can fight the physical battle around you, you must first fight the spiritual battle against Satan that's going on inside of you. Before you can truly defend others, you must firmly believe in the cause you're fighting for. You have to realize that you will almost certainly be persecuted for doing what is right. But you must ignore the voice inside you that tells you it's not worth it. Christ left His heavenly throne and became the very lowest of men for us. Christ paid the ultimate price for our freedom from sin. Should we then not give of ourselves to defend the freedom of others?"

Grace sat silently listening to Reverend Carver preach. He said just the right words at just the right moment. Grace was moved by his sermon and knew she needed to trust God and believe that He was able to soften even the hardest of hearts, including her father's.

As the words of the sermon touched Grace's heart, she began to remember some of her concerns from the last few years. *What if Father never changes? Will he ever get saved? Will I ever be able to marry David?* These thoughts had consumed her for so long. Now, as she sat listening to Reverend Carver, all those doubts slipped away, and her hopes were aroused.

"Our cause is not a worthless one. We are defending those who are unable to defend themselves. This is exactly what Christ did for us. He saved us when we couldn't save ourselves. In Matthew 5: 11-12, Christ says, 'Blessed are ye when people shall insult you, persecute you, and falsely say all manner of evil against you for my sake. Rejoice and be exceedingly glad because great is your reward in heaven, for so persecuted they the prophets who were before you.' Christ tells us that persecution is not something new. It has been going on since the beginning of time. If they persecuted Christ, will they not also persecute us? Yes. And even though we may not be rewarded for our persecution here on earth, Christ tells us that we *will* be rewarded in heaven.

"My family and I have been persecuted for doing what's right. Even though we left for a time, we are here to stay. We will not leave again no matter what persecution might come. God has given me a task: To speak the truth, and I will continue to do so. He's given me leadership over you, and a good leader does not leave his people in times of trouble. I want you to know that I will do my best to fulfill my duties as a husband, father, leader, and God's ambassador. He will not be mocked by the words of foolish men!"

When Reverend Carver was coming to a close, a man who had been standing outside the church near the back window quickly and quietly left. This man was not a member of the congregation. He had not come for the purpose of learning more about the Scriptures. He was there on other business about which no one knew. If anyone had known his business, they would have surely spoken up. But no one noticed him, no one except for Reverend Carver, who watched him leave.

After the sermon, everyone shook Reverend Carver's hands and told him how much they enjoyed the sermon and welcomed him home. They also thanked Reverend Smith for all his work over the past few years.

*   *   *

"So, what happened? Did anyone see you?"

"No one saw me. I stood outside the back window. I heard every word."

"What'd he say?"

"He was preaching alright…on the war."

"Hasn't that man learned anything? I thought the barn burning would be enough!"

"I don't think he's scared. He seems pretty convinced that what he's doing is right. He says he won't stop no matter what harm might come."

"We'll see about that! He's got it coming to him now."

"What are you thinking?"

"We can't storm the church. It would create too much of a stir. We'll have to do it in secret; keep it as quiet as possible."

"What do you mean?"

"We'll kill him!"

"What? Don't you think that's a little extreme?"

"No! Thomas lost his life fighting for our cause. Now Carver's gonna die for his!"

"When?"

"I'll round up some of the boys tomorrow." The man paused as he looked at his companion. "You're having second thoughts?"

"No…no I'm in."

"Good. Meet me at the blacksmith's shop tomorrow morning, and we'll come up with a plan. You'll be there, Tom?"

"I'll be there."

*   *   *

"Wasn't that sermon great?" Grace asked her mother on their ride home.

"Yes. He's a fine speaker. God has truly gifted him. I'd say that was the best sermon he's ever given."

"It opened my eyes," Grace related. "All the doubts that I've ever had slipped away. I'm not afraid anymore. I realize that suffering is normal. I mean, Christ suffered for doing what was right, and so will we. Our cause is worth defending. We just need to keep trusting the Lord."

"I'm glad that God has strengthened your faith, Grace. And yes, our cause is a worthy one. We're standing up for others. The Negros are just as good as whites and just as in need of a Savior. Let this be your witnessing field, Grace. Never be ashamed to do what's right."

When they arrived back home, Grace and Mrs. Johnson noticed that Mr. Johnson wasn't anywhere to be found.

"Where's Father?" Grace asked.

"I don't know. Usually he's here waiting for us."

Just then, Mr. Johnson walked in the door. He looked uneasy.

"Are you all right, Tom?" Mrs. Johnson asked.

"I'm fine."

He paused slightly, feeling uncomfortable. Barn burning was one thing; killing someone was another. His spirit was restless, and his conscious had finally been awakened.

"I have to go feed the animals," he mumbled dryly, trying to escape the curious glances of his wife and daughter. He quickly walked out of the house.

"That was strange," Mrs. Johnson commented. She went about fixing lunch.

Grace, however, walked out to the barn. It was rare to see her father in this type of condition.

"Father, is everything alright?" Grace asked as Mr. Johnson fed the animals.

"Yes, Grace, everything's fine. Just go back inside with your mother."

"I know something's troubling you."

"I said, 'I'm fine!'"

Grace turned around and headed back inside the house.

"He's gotta pay! He's had enough chances! John just lost his son for the Confederate cause, and it was men like Timothy who killed him! He's gotta pay!" Mr. Johnson kept telling himself. Mr. Miller had reeled him in with all his lies, and Mr. Johnson had taken the bait. Now he found it difficult to get away. He tried to push his convictions aside, not knowing where they might lead.

The following day, Mr. Johnson told his wife that he was going to run into town.

"Oh, good, that saves me a trip," Mrs. Johnson replied. "Here's a list of some things I need from the mercantile."

"I don't know if I'll have time—"

"I can go, Mother. I'll pick up the items you need while Father's doing his business," Grace offered.

"Well, if you want to, Grace, I see no reason why you can't go. Are you alright with it, Tom?"

Mr. Johnson hesitated, not wanting them to know of his doings. But on the other hand, he did not want their curiosity to be aroused if he refused.

"Alright, Grace, you can come."

Grace smiled and took the list of items from her mother. Then, Grace and Mr. Johnson hopped into the wagon, and their little cabin was soon out of sight.

Together they rode into town. Grace couldn't remember the last time when she and her father had spent time together, just the two of them. Grace knew her father was wrong, but she still loved him a great deal. Even though he had not let her marry David, Grace knew that he was only trying to seek the very best for her, even if his interpretation of "best" differed from hers and her mother's.

"Alright, run into the mercantile and pick those things up for your mother," he told her. "I'll be with you shortly."

"Yes, sir." She quickly headed over to the mercantile.

"How are you, Grace?" Mrs. Lawson, the mercantile owner, asked.

"Very well, thank you. I just have a few things to pick up," Grace responded, handing Mrs. Lawson the list.

"I'll grab those for you."

Grace smiled and walked around the store, looking at all the beautiful merchandise. A dress caught her eye, and she headed over to the window where it was displayed. She loved the beautiful lace that adorned it and the little pearls sewed along the neckline. Just then, something caught her attention outside of the store. She noticed her father. He was at the blacksmith's shop, talking with Mr. Miller and four other men. Mr. Miller's countenance was grave, and he looked set on getting something done. They all headed inside the shop where the shadows cast by the walls concealed their figures.

Something's not right, Grace thought to herself.

"Here you are, Grace." Mrs. Lawson handed Grace the bag of items.

"Oh, thank you, Mrs. Lawson. How much do I owe you?"

"Two dollars."

Grace pulled out the money from her purse and gave it to Mrs. Lawson.

"Thank you, Grace. Have a nice day."

"You, too, Mrs. Lawson."

Grace walked across the street to the blacksmith's shop. The men must have seen her coming, for their conversation quickly came to an end. Mr. Miller resumed his work, the other men left, and Mr. Johnson and Grace rode away.

"Is that all you had to come into town for?" Grace questioned.

"We just had to talk about a few things," he casually responded.

Grace knew it wasn't respectful to continually ask questions, so she decided not to say anything else.

* * *

Later that night, the Johnsons were sitting around the dinner table when Mr. Johnson excused himself.

"Where are you going?" Mrs. Johnson inquired.

"I have to head over to, uh, Clark's place."

"At this hour?"

"It shouldn't take too long. I'll be back shortly," he calmly replied as if nothing abnormal was going on.

"Alright."

He walked outside, and Mrs. Johnson started to clear the table.

Grace watched her father from the kitchen window. She caught sight of something that made her uneasy.

"Something's wrong," she worriedly commented.

"What do you mean?"

"Father just grabbed his gun."

She continued to watch her father as he rode over the hill towards the Carvers'. The Carvers' cabin was in the opposite direction of Mr. Clark's.

Suddenly, Grace remembered the brief meeting her father had had with Mr. Miller earlier that morning.

"Oh, no!" Grace exclaimed.

"What is it?"

"Father's headed towards the Carvers!" Grace turned toward her mother. "Today, I saw him talking with Mr. Miller in town. They looked like—" Grace stopped short. Her breath quickened. "They're gonna kill him! They're gonna kill Mr. Carver! That's why Father grabbed his gun!"

"Are you sure about this, Grace?"

"Positive! That's why they ended their conversation so quickly when I came over! This explains everything!"

She quickly dashed outside, saddled up Violet, and was just about to ride off when Mrs. Johnson grabbed the reins.

"I'm coming with you!"

"No, Ma, please, stay here! This is something I need to do by myself. I don't think they'll hurt me."

Grasping the reins even tighter, Mrs. Johnson stated, "Grace, when people's consciences have been seared, they're able to do the most unthinkable things! If John Miller is able to kill an innocent preacher, I don't know what would stop him from killing you, too."

"Father would never let him do that. I have to try, Ma!"

Mrs. Johnson paused. She knew she couldn't keep her daughter from doing this. So with a nervous spirit, she slowly released the reins.

"Alright, but be careful, Grace! Men with quick tempers are quick to do harm. They have guns!"

"And I have God!"

CHAPTER 13

COURAGE AND CONVERSION

The wind swept across Grace's face as she pressed Violet to go faster. Her heart raced.

Once Grace arrived, she yanked on the reins, and Violet came to a halt. Six horses were tied up outside the cabin; the men were there. She could hear talking coming from inside.

"Oh, God, help me!" she cried to the only One who could possibly save her from the danger that lay inside the cabin.

She ran into the house. The tip of John Miller's gun was pointed right at Mr. Carver, who stood in a protective position in front of his wife and son. David was embracing Mrs. Carver, whose eyes were wide with fear.

"Stop!" Grace shouted.

All the men turned around to look at her.

"Grace!" David exclaimed.

"What do you think you're doing?" Grace questioned them all with her glance particularly focused on Mr. Miller.

"I should think it's obvious!" came the gruff reply from Mr. Miller. "Tom, tell your daughter to go home!"

Mr. Johnson walked over to Grace and looked down into her determined young face.

"What are you doing here, Grace?" he asked her.

"I couldn't let you do this!"

A haughty laugh broke out from Mr. Miller.

"And you think you could stop me?"

"I by myself can do nothing, but I'm not alone," Grace declared boldly.

"You brought others? Where are they?" Mr. Miller inquired.

"I didn't bring others; I brought One, One who is stronger than all of you!"

"Who?"

"God."

Immediately Mr. Miller and the other four men burst out laughing. Mr. Johnson, however, was silent.

"God? What is he going to do? Strike me down with lightning?" Mr. Miller sarcastically snipped.

"He is able to do whatever He pleases," Mr. Carver answered.

"Quiet, Carver!" Mr. Miller bellowed, his eyes wide with fury.

"You can't kill Mr. Carver," Grace firmly declared as she silently offered up another prayer.

"You can't stop me, and neither can your god!"

"Yes, He can. He can change lives, soften the hardest of hearts."

"Oh, and you think He could soften mine and make me forget all about this, forget about all this blasted preacher has done?" Mr. Miller roared.

"You wouldn't forget, but you'd feel differently about it. You'd see that Mr. Carver is defending those who can't defend themselves. You'd see that color doesn't affect a person's value, and you'd see that killing an innocent human being is wrong!"

"'Innocent?' My Thomas lost his life fighting stupid people like him!" he screamed, pointing a gnarled finger at Mr. Carver.

"And countless other young sons have lost their lives

fighting people like you!" Grace shouted back. "Mr. Carver has just as much freedom to say what he believes as you do, and yet you don't see him barging into your house with a group of armed men, threatening to kill you!"

Mr. Miller slowly walked towards Grace.

"Human life is valuable," Grace pronounced.

"Oh, it is? Not the lives of troublemakers like him! They're better off getting cut down right away, and that's exactly what I should have done four years ago!"

Aiming his gun at Mr. Carver, Mr. Miller was just about to pull the trigger when someone called out, "No!" This time, it wasn't Grace's voice protesting.

Mr. Miller stopped.

"Tom! Get out of the way!" he hollered.

"No!" Mr. Johnson fiercely shouted back.

"What's gotten into you?" Mr. Miller asked angrily.

"Sense, that's what! Grace is right! He hasn't done anything to us!"

"Not done anything? Thomas is dead!"

"Timothy didn't kill him!"

"He didn't, but it was men like him who did! Thomas is dead, and I'm not getting him back!"

"That's not Timothy's fault. Grace is right. He has just as much freedom to speak his opinion as we do."

"He speaks with words, and I speak with my gun!"

"That's not the way to solve your problems!"

"Well, nothing else works!"

"Have you ever tried any other way? Hatred will just make this war last longer; it won't bring it to an end." Mr. Johnson turned towards his daughter. "Grace has been right all along.

I didn't see it, but now I do. I don't want to live in hatred anymore! This life is hard enough as it is without everyone always looking for ways to disagree."

Then, Mr. Johnson held up his gun and boldly proclaimed, "My gun won't speak for me!" With that, he threw his gun on the floor.

Mr. Miller looked at Mr. Johnson in shock. The other men stood, looking at one another. Then, slowly, one by one, they also threw down their guns.

"You're all insane!" Mr. Miller shouted.

"If you kill Timothy, you'll have to kill me, too," Mr. Johnson declared, standing even taller than before. Then, without a word, the other men lined up in front of the Carvers, shielding them all from Mr. Miller.

"It's over, John. Let the man be," Mr. Johnson stated firmly.

Mr. Miller backed away. He scowled at them all and gave a particularly nasty look to Mr. Johnson. Then, he angrily left the house and rode off. Slowly, the other men left, leaving the Carvers, Grace, and Mr. Johnson alone in the cabin.

Grace looked up at her father, and he looked down at her. She smiled at him, and he smiled back.

"You're a pretty special girl, Grace," he proudly told his brave daughter.

"God gave me the courage, Father. Although, I have to be honest that when I first came in I felt like fainting." She chuckled, and he did, too.

"Grace." David walked over, a look of shock on his face. "I—" he couldn't seem to finish.

Grace looked into his eyes and placed a gentle hand on

his shoulder.

"You know you could have been killed," David finally managed to say.

"I know that. But I couldn't sit by and do nothing. And remember, I didn't do it alone. God was watching out for all of us."

"Thank you, God!" David sighed a sigh of relief, and he hugged Grace.

Mr. Carver walked closer to Mr. Johnson.

"I want to thank you," he told him. "You saved my life."

"It's the least I could have done after—" Mr. Johnson paused, his past weighing heavily on him as he pondered the words he knew he must say.

"There's something you need to know." He paused, feeling as if he was going to choke on his next words. He lowered his eyes to the floor, unable to look Mr. Carver in the eyes.

"I burnt your barn."

A gasp escaped Grace's lips, and the Carvers stood staring at Mr. Johnson in shock. No one spoke. What could they say? How could they put their feelings into words? The same man who stood before them, the man who had just saved their lives was also the man who had caused them so much heartache?

Mr. Carver felt some anger creep up inside of him, and yet he couldn't bring himself to say anything to rebuke Mr. Johnson for what he had done. His anger slowly subsided as he realized how lost he, too, had been before he had come to know Christ.

"I won't ask for your forgiveness. What I did was unforgivable," Mr. Johnson quietly confessed, his face still towards the ground.

Mr. Carver placed a gentle hand on Mr. Johnson's shoulder.

"God commands us to forgive, Tom," Mr. Carver told the brokenhearted man. "I forgive you."

Mr. Johnson's gaze left the floor when Mr. Carver said those three words.

"How…how could you? I've been so awful to you and your family…to my family. Why would anyone forgive me?"

"We've all done bad things in our lives, Tom, but God forgives us. He loves us, and He wants us to follow Him."

"I don't think He'd want me."

"It's sinners Jesus came to save, Tom. He came to earth, died on a cross, and rose again three days later so we could one day live in heaven forever with Him."

There was a dramatic pause as Mr. Johnson and Mr. Carver locked eyes.

"He wants you," Mr. Carver continued.

A tear slowly rolled down Mr. Johnson's cheek.

"Then I want Him. I see Him in Grace and Clara. There's something about them that's different."

"Christ shines through in our lives, Tom. People may pretend not to notice, but they do. Will I see you in church on Sunday?"

Mr. Johnson hesitated then nodded.

"I'll be there."

Mr. Carver smiled and then turned his attention to Grace.

"Grace is a fine young lady."

"Yes, she is," Mr. Johnson agreed.

He walked over to Grace and David and to everyone's surprise announced, "You're a fine man, David. I wouldn't want to entrust my Grace to anyone else. If you still want her,

I'll give you my blessing."

Grace gasped in surprise, and David played those words over in his mind, wondering if they were real.

"I do, sir!" he proclaimed.

Grace smiled the biggest smile and wrapped her arms around her father's neck.

"Thank you, Father! Thank you!"

"You deserve each other, Grace. I'm sorry I ever held anything against him."

"He's not mad at you, Father, and neither am I. We've been praying for you all along."

"Well, your prayers have been answered."

CHAPTER 14

PLANNING

That Sunday, Mr. Johnson did go to church, just as he said he would. It was the first church service he had ever attended and on a very special day, at that. The Civil War had ended.

Mrs. Johnson was in awe of the change in her husband. This is what she had prayed for for years. Now the day had finally come: her husband was attending church. And who would have ever thought that he would have become a Christian? The previous night, Mr. Johnson had come to know Christ as his Savior.

"Is this really happening?" Grace asked her mother as she stood next to her, watching her father get baptized.

"I can't believe it, either, Grace. I've been praying for years for this day to come, and now that it's here, it doesn't seem real." They both looked at each other and smiled.

After the service, everyone came up to congratulate Mr. Johnson. Husbands, wives, and children all wanted to share their joy.

"Why don't you and your family join us for lunch? I made enough lemon chicken to feed an army!" Mrs. Jones, Anna's mother, told Mrs. Johnson.

"That'd be wonderful, Renee! Thank you!"

* * *

"So, you're finally engaged?" Anna asked Grace as they walked together outside after lunch.

"Yes."

"Are you excited?"

"Yes, a little nervous, though," Grace confessed.

"Why?"

"Well, it's going to be a whole new life."

"Yes, but a wonderful one!" Anna exclaimed.

"I know." Grace smiled.

"Grace, I have some exciting news, too," Anna stated.

"What is it?"

"I'm engaged to Jonathan Koch."

"That's wonderful! When did he ask you?"

"About a week ago. We're planning on having the wedding mid-July."

"That's not far off at all!"

"Well, we didn't want to wait. Say, have you and David settled on a date, yet?"

"No, but if I know David, he'll want to do it soon. After all, we *have* been waiting for over four years!"

"Would you like to make it a double wedding?"

"What?"

"Oh, it'd be wonderful!" Anna proclaimed. "After all, almost everyone who will be attending your wedding will be attending mine. The only other people would be family, and it would be a great opportunity to meet each other's relatives!"

"Well, I'm sure David will be fine with it. That's sounds like a great idea."

"You talk to him about it, and let me know."

"I'll do that."

They hugged each other, and then Anna added, "I can't believe it! It seems like just yesterday we were talking about our dreams for the future. Now, they're finally happening!"

Grace talked to David about Anna's idea for a double

wedding, and he gave his approval. So the date was set: July 11 at three o'clock. Grace and Anna were to have a double wedding, and it wasn't going to be any small affair!

* * *

There were lots of things to do before the big day: Send out invitations to the various people, decide what the menu would be for dinner, what kind of cake, and who everyone would be in the wedding.

"I'm leaving the ring bearer and groomsmen up to you, Anna. I don't have any brothers," Grace told her friend.

"I think Ethan, Luke, and Matthew should be the groomsmen, and Grant should be the ring bearer."

"That's sounds good to me," Grace agreed.

"Who should be the Maid of Honor?" Anna asked.

"Mary. Then, Katelyn and my cousins Chloe and Margaret can be the bridesmaids."

"Great idea!"

"Alright, so that leaves the flower girl. Do you want junior bridesmaids? I have a few more cousins who would love to be in the wedding."

"What have we got to lose? The more the merrier!"

"Alright, then. My cousins Abigail and Lydia can be the junior bridesmaids and Elizabeth can be the flower girl. I think that's it," Grace declared.

"It seems we have everything worked out."

"Yes, I think we do."

"I assume your mother will be making her famous rhubarb pie?"

"Most definitely, along with her delicious banana chocolate pie! Guess how many pies she said she'd make?"

"How many?"

"Ten."

"What? Ten pies?" Anna asked in disbelief.

"Everyone in my family goes crazy over them. My father himself could eat a whole one!"

"I know, but ten?"

"Well, after all, it's going to be your family, my family, and all of our friends."

"That's true. But one woman baking ten pies? You should start praying for her!" Both of them burst out laughing.

"I already have! I offered to help her, but she said she wants to do everything."

"I suppose all mothers are like that when their daughters are getting married."

"Probably."

"Oh, by the way, my mother and aunt are going to bake some things, too. I believe she said cookies and apple turnovers. Mrs. Alden offered to help with dinner," Anna related.

"Oh, good! And we said fried chicken, baked potatoes, green beans, and bread, right?"

"Right!"

"I think this is going to be the best meal I've ever had in my whole life!" Grace jubilantly proclaimed.

"I think this is going to be the best day I've ever had in my whole life!"

"I hope everything goes alright. I'm afraid I'll faint with all those people staring at me!"

"Relax, you'll be fine! Besides, you won't be the only one whom they'll be staring at."

"Oh, I see how this is! You just wanted to make this a

double wedding so that more people would get to gaze upon your beautiful self," Grace teased.

"Absolutely!" Anna chuckled.

They both loved having a friend they could play around with. Together, they headed outside and went over their plans one more time just for the fun of it.

"Hey, look!" Grace exclaimed. "There's that creek that we used to play in on our family picnics."

"Oh, I'd forgotten all about it."

Suddenly, Anna started chuckling, and just a few seconds later, she was beside herself laughing. She couldn't seem to stop.

"What are you laughing at?" Grace asked.

"I just remembered the time when I pushed you in, and you fell flat on your face. You came out soaking wet, covered in mud!" She continued laughing. "You must have chased me halfway to Mississippi!'"

"Ha, ha, ha," Grace said sarcastically. "Very funny."

Then, an idea popped into her head.

"I can't believe it!" she exclaimed.

"What?" Anna asked.

"That flower on the other side of the creek; it's one of the rarest ones in Virginia!"

"It just looks like a normal wildflower to me."

"Of course it's not just a normal wildflower! It's a pegonia!"

"A pegonia?"

"They're one of the rarest kinds of flowers in America. I just read about them. Come on, let's get a closer look!" Grace urged.

They walked down the bank, and there on the other side

of the creek sat the pegonia.

"I'll jump over to the other side, and then I'll help you across. I'm a better jumper than you are," Grace antagonized.

"Says who?" Anna asked defensively.

"Please, Anna, don't try to argue with plain facts," she teased.

Grace jumped over the creek and landed safely on the other side.

"Come on, you can do it. I'll help you!" she exclaimed.

Anna walked back a little ways to get a head start. She ran, jumped, and just made it to the other side. However, the slippery mud caused her to lose her balance. Grace slowly let Anna's hand slip from her grip, and Anna landed right in the creek. Grace started laughing hysterically. Anna's blond hair was soaked with muddy water.

"Oh, stop laughing and help me out!" Anna insisted.

Grace extended her hand to help Anna out, but Anna quickly yanked it, pulling Grace into the creek with her.

"Not so funny now, is it?" Anna sneered.

Grace looked at Anna, covered in muddy water, and Anna looked at Grace, covered just as much as she was. They both burst out laughing.

"A pegonia? Really?" Anna joked.

"It was the best I could think of!"

"Well," Anna concluded, "I suppose there's only one thing to do."

She stood up, acting as if she was going to get out of the creek. She quickly spun around and splashed water at Grace. Grace, surprised, quickly stood up and splashed water right back. They stood there in the creek, splashing water until they were both completely soaked. They might have been getting older, but they refused to grow up!

CHAPTER 15

THE WAR RAGES ON

The big day finally arrived. Everyone was bustling to get things done. Mrs. Johnson kept finding more things to do.

"This needs to be put here, and these need to be over there. And you know what? These flowers would probably look even prettier if they were on that table over there," Mrs. Johnson told herself.

"Everything is going to be great, Ma. You've done a wonderful job planning this. Really, you don't have to worry."

"I know, Grace. But it's not every day your daughter gets married."

"Lots of girls have gotten married, Ma."

"Well, not you, and I want everything to be perfect."

"It will be. You couldn't get a better wedding than this. You and Mrs. Jones have done an incredible amount of work, and I don't want you to do one thing more for me. After all, you have to enjoy this day, too."

"I suppose you're right, dear."

"Now, you give me those flowers, and I'll set them on whatever table you want."

Mrs. Johnson handed Grace the vase of flowers and instructed her on what table to put them. Grace set them down on the head table.

She turned around to see her mother quickly rearrange something on one of the tables.

"Ma!"

"What? The napkin wasn't folded properly."

"Ma, please. You don't have to change anything else. Everything looks wonderful."

"Fine. I won't change one more thing."

"Good. Now I'm going inside to get dressed for the wedding." Grace headed towards the house.

"Oh, let me help you, dear! The buttons on that dress are a bit stubborn," Mrs. Johnson quickly called after her.

Mrs. Johnson hovered over Grace nonstop. She made sure Grace's veil was sitting just right upon her head of flowing brown curls. She adjusted the string of pearls that beautifully adorned Grace's neck and put on Grace's shoes for her. Finally, after an hour of constant movement and fretting, Mrs. Johnson sat down on Grace's bed. Admiring the beautiful image of her soon-to-be-wed daughter, she exclaimed proudly, "You look beautiful, Grace!"

"It's the dress, Ma. Thank you so much for letting me wear it."

"I wanted you to, Grace. And now it's yours to pass on to your daughter someday."

"Oh, Ma, I couldn't. It's too beautiful. You have to keep it."

"No, now not another word about it. It's yours to keep, and that's that."

Grace smiled at her glowing mother, and beheld her image in the mirror. She swished the dress back and forth.

"I bet you looked radiant in it," Grace told her mother.

"Oh, not nearly as pretty as you!"

"You give yourself far too little credit, Ma."

Mrs. Johnson started to blush.

"Oh, you," she said, embarrassed.

"Well, you are! I bet all the young men around must have fallen for you."

"Well, I did have a couple beaus but none like your father. He thought I was "'the prettiest girl this side of the Mississippi!'"

"He said that to you?"

"He most certainly did on the night of our wedding. Just knowing that he thought I was beautiful made me happy enough."

"Well, I hope David thinks the same."

"Oh, he does, dear, believe me."

"How do you know?"

"I can tell by the way he looks at you. There's a gleam in a man's eyes when he's around the woman he loves, and mothers spot it very easily. After all, we were young women once, too. Your father had that same gleam in his eyes, and I used to light up whenever I saw it. It made me know how much he really cared about me."

"That's so sweet."

"It is. And you're very blessed, Grace."

"Why?"

"Because you and David both have something very special: David knows that you've never given your heart away to anyone else, and you know the same about him. He's reserved his heart only for you, and you've reserved yours only for him. That makes your relationship all the more special, and you'll find that it will bind you two even closer."

"I never thought about it that way before."

"God blesses us when we love the way He wants us to love, and He will bless you and David for your faithfulness to

Him in that you've both guarded your minds and your hearts and saved your love for each other."

Grace was now seated on the bed beside her mother. She wrapped her arms around her and whispered into her ear, "I love you, Ma."

"I love you too, Grace."

*   *   *

The wedding was a grand affair. Mrs. Johnson and Mrs. Jones had done everything possible to make this a beautiful and lively event. Ribbons adorned the pews, and beautiful bouquets of wildflowers adorned the windowsills. As the many family members and close friends filed into the church, Mrs. Johnson and Mrs. Jones were showered with compliments on the remarkable decorations.

After the ceremony there was a nice reception at the Johnsons'. There was supper and soon afterwards dessert. Everyone ate to their heart's content. Mothers tried in vain to control their children. Grace spotted her cousins Jacob, Samuel, and Jonah hiding underneath the dessert table, sneakily snatching cookies while their mother was preoccupied with the three younger children. Katelyn's younger brothers Micah and Mason and their friends Judah and Caleb were also trying to sneak desserts, but their mothers caught them red-handed. The children frowned and returned the sweets to the table. Grace quietly chuckled to herself.

"Tom, isn't that your third piece of pie?" Mrs. Johnson questioned her husband as he resumed his place next to her at the head table.

Since Mr. Johnson's conversion, he and Mrs. Johnson had grown even closer. Mr. Johnson was now filled with the joy and love of Christ, which greatly changed the way he treated his wife.

"Yes, and you should take it as a compliment!" he stated.

"I do, Tom. It's just, aren't you going to get sick?" Mrs. Johnson asked.

"I could never get sick from eating your desserts, especially your pies."

Not surprisingly, by the end of the evening, all of Mrs. Johnson's pies were gone.

*   *   *

"How are you, MRS. Carver?" Anna asked Grace as they sat at the head table, eating their desserts. Their parents sat across from them, happily engaged in a conversation with one another while David and Jonathan were standing by the dessert table, consumed in a conversation of their own. This gave Grace and Anna time to converse peacefully, just the two of them.

"Very well, thank you, MRS. Koch," Grace cheerfully responded.

"Can you believe this? We're married women, now!"

"I know. It doesn't seem possible."

"Doesn't it make the wedding all the more special knowing the war is finally over? After four long years, it has ended. I'm so happy."

"I am, too, but you know, in a sense, war never ends. Every day we need to fight the battle against temptation in our own lives and stand strong in our faith. Satan is always looking for ways to get us to stumble and turn away from the truth. We have to do what's right, no matter what's going on around us, and God will bless us for our obedience and faithfulness to

Him. My mother and I were actually just talking about that before the wedding."

"You know, you're right. I never thought about it before. We have to keep fighting the good fight even when things get rough."

Grace nodded.

"The physical war is over, and I'm so glad it is, but the spiritual war in our daily lives rages on," Grace stated as Anna grasped her hand and smiled.

And so, the war rages on in all of our lives until the one true Victor returns: Jesus Christ, our King, our Lord, and our God! May you be inspired to stand up for Christ and live your life in full service to Him!

SCRIPTURE REFERENCES

Note from the Author: I added these verses as a help to the reader. They deal with some of the main biblical issues and lessons presented in *The War Rages On*.

BEAUTY/PURITY

Proverbs 4:23 – Keep your heart with all diligence, for out of it spring the issues of life.

Proverbs 31:30 - Charm is deceitful and beauty is passing, but a woman who fears the LORD, she shall be praised.

Matthew 5:8 - Blessed are the pure in heart, for they shall see God.

FAITH/TRUSTING THE LORD

Psalm 28:7 - The LORD is my strength and my shield; my heart trusted in Him, and I am helped; therefore my heart greatly rejoices, and with my song I will praise Him.

Proverbs 3:5-6 - Trust in the LORD with all your heart, and lean not on your own understanding; in all your ways acknowledge Him, and He shall direct your paths.

Hebrews 11:6 - But without faith it is impossible to please Him, for he who comes to God must believe that He is, and that He is a rewarder of those who diligently seek Him.

PERSECUTION

John 15:18-19 - If the world hates you, you know that it hated Me before it hated you. If you were of the world, the world would love its own. Yet because you are not of the world, but I chose you out of the world, therefore the world hates you.

FORGIVENESS/LOVING YOUR ENEMIES

Matthew 5:43-45 - You have heard that it was said, 'You shall love your neighbor and hate your enemy.' But I say to you, love your enemies, bless those who curse you, do good to those who hate you, and pray for those who spitefully use you and persecute you, that you may be sons of your Father in heaven; for He makes His sun rise on the evil and on the good, and sends rain on the just and on the unjust.

Ephesians 4:32 – And be kind to one another, tenderhearted, forgiving one another, even as God in Christ forgave you.

STANDING UP FOR CHRIST/COURAGE

Psalm 27:1 - The LORD is my light and my salvation; whom shall I fear? The LORD is the strength of my life; of whom shall I be afraid?

Matthew 5:16 - Let your light so shine before men, that they may see your good works and glorify your Father in heaven.

Matthew 10:28 – And do not fear those who kill the body but cannot kill the soul. But rather fear Him who is able to destroy both soul and body in hell.

Romans 8:31 - What then shall we say to these things? If God is for us, who can be against us?

TRIALS/SUFFERING

Romans 5:3-4 – And not only that, but we also glory in tribulations, knowing that tribulation produces perseverance; and perseverance, character; and character, hope.

Romans 8:28 - And we know that all things work together for good to those who love God, to those who are the called according to His purpose.

James 1:2-4 – My brethren, count it all joy when you fall into various trials, knowing that the testing of your faith produces patience. But let patience have its perfect work, that you may be perfect and complete, lacking nothing.

SALVATION

John 3:16 - For God so loved the world that He gave His only begotten Son, that whoever believes in Him should not perish but have everlasting life.

Romans 5:1-2 - Therefore, having been justified by faith, we have peace with God through our Lord Jesus Christ, through whom also we have access by faith into this grace in which we stand, and rejoice in hope of the glory of God.

Romans 5:8 - But God demonstrates His own love toward us, in that while we were still sinners, Christ died for us.

Romans 10:9 – that if you confess with your mouth the Lord Jesus and believe in your heart that God has raised Him from the dead, you will be saved.

O Beautiful Freedom

Arr. Julia LoVullo

Cecelia Schmidt

2015